The God Stone

The God Stone

Part Three in the Cold Days Series

James Howerton

www.iuniverse.com

THE GOD STONE
PART THREE IN THE COLD DAYS SERIES

This is a work of fiction. All of the characters, names, incidents, organizations, and dialogue in this novel are either the products of the author's imagination or are used fictitiously.

iUniverse books may be ordered through booksellers or by contacting:

iUniverse LLC
1663 Liberty Drive
Bloomington, IN 47403
www.iuniverse.com
1-800-Authors (1-800-288-4677)

ISBN: 978-1-4917-3745-3 (sc)
ISBN: 978-1-4917-3744-6 (e)

Library of Congress Control Number: 2014910952

Printed in the United States of America.

iUniverse rev. date: 06/16/2014

"For my good friend and neighbor, Randy."

One . . .

Mira's pet wolf came loping into the camp of the Tolai just in time, as the Four Tribes of the mountain people were packed up and preparing to haul the bison meat back to the western peaks.

Mira cried with relief. Several days ago they had survived the worst storm Mira had ever seen, a black monster of sky that swept death across these Short Hills of the east. The big grey dog had disappeared in the storm and had not been seen since.

"Oh, my Wolf!"

Mira, daughter of Etain, chieftain of the Tolai, knelt down in the tall grass and hugged the great dog. "I thought you were lost, Wolf. I thought I would never see you again."

Mira's mate, Thais, of the savage tribe of Menkala and now an adapted Tolai, knelt beside her and rubbed Wolf as the dog joyfully splashed his face, it's silver tail rowing the wind.

"I think you knew we were leaving for the mountains," Thais said to the dog. "I think you have been watching us."

"Why would he do that? Why would he hide himself like that?"

"Look out there, Mira." Thais aimed his hand at the grass plains north. "Why Wolf disappeared."

Mira stared, but could see nothing at first. Then suddenly a white drop appeared over the grass. "What is it?"

"She-wolf," Thais said. "Wolf found a mate. I wondered when he would."

Mira stared and did make out the head of a large wolf; but it was pure white, like no other wolf Mira had seen. "Wolf found a mate," she marveled. "What will happen now?"

"They will either follow the she-wolf's life and you will have to say farewell to Wolf; or they will decide Wolf's life, and they will follow us back to the mountains."

"I can't say farewell," Mira said, hugging her big pet. "What do you think, Thais?"

"I believe they will follow us. We have free food and protection for them, and wolves are not fools. Sooner than you think the dona will come into camp. And one day Shana will have wolf pups to play with and raise."

"I pray that's it's so." She stared at the white dog-head peering up from the grass at the camp, at her new mate. The dona's eyes shone red in the moonlight. "A white wolf. Dona; that is the Menkala word for wolf."

"Male wolf is dono, female wolf is dona."

"That will be her name then," Mira said. "I will give you a big chunk of bison, Wolf—but you'd better share with Dona. We have to make her welcome."

"Feed Wolf first, and when he is full, give him the bison and he will take it to her." Thais watched the dona in the grass, her eyes fearful and alert. "White wolf is an omen to the Menkala; they will not kill a white wolf."

"Maybe she will be a good omen to us."

As Mira fed a ravenous Wolf, the Conai hunter Golthis, called Giant of the South Mountain, strode into camp. He was a colossal man, very ugly—(in the battle with the Menkala he had lost an eye, and now wore a patch over it, sewn by his mate Jella, who had found the torn out eye unacceptable).

Mira smiled up at him. "My cousin," she said. "How is Jella?"

"She complains of these Short Hills," Golthis replied. "Her heart aches for home—she's meaner to me than usual." Golthis frowned down at Wolf, who was gobbling precious bison meat. "So the creature has returned. I'd hoped we were rid of it."

"Wolf has returned," Mira said. "And he brings a mate with him. Look out there."

Golthis aimed his good eye to the north. "A white wolf?"

"Thais says it means good luck."

Golthis grunted. "What it means is more of those scavengers in the tribe. A she-wolf can make a great many demon pups."

Thais approached and embraced the giant. "Are the Conai packed up?"

"And very eager to get out of here, before another of those storms blows in; before the Menkala sniff us out."

"They are far to the east, trying to deal with the Paw-Nee."

"And we have company of our own. My scouts spotted many of the Snake People along the stream to the south."

"That's good," Thais said. "The Menkala will find out that we have made friends with the desert tribes. It will enrage them, but make them think twice."

"Still, there are too many tribes out here. Give me the mountains and fewer neighbors."

Just days ago the chieftains of the Four Mountain Tribes had met with chieftains of the desert tribes; together they had smoked the dried leaves of the spear-head plant, and formed a pact of peace and mutual cooperation in the hunting of the bison that roamed the Short Hills by the millions.

"Snake people," Golthis grumped. "I question those who worship snakes."

"Our comrades now. And I wouldn't call them Snake People; they take offense to that. They are the Ooma."

"They're a skinny people; if they are attacked or we are, I hope they fight and don't run away."

"They will fight," Thais said. "They are distance fighters. It's said that with a sling they will knock the brains out of a man from a good far away."

"Well, I would prefer to keep what brains I have. And I suppose there are enough bison for the both of us."

Despite the devastating storm, the Four Tribes—Salotai, Conai, Tolai and Emotai—had made a spectacular hunt, and had staggering loads of bison meat and furs to haul back home. The terrible warriors of these plains, the Southern Menkala, were far away, and the Northern Menkala rarely ventured this far south of the Flat River. Thais was satisfied that they would safely get the loads of bison home before the Cold Days brought snow in to seal the mountain valleys.

Wolf let out a loud burp and Mira, laughing, gave him a big chunk of bison. Wolf immediately snatched it from her and trotted off to feed his new mate.

"Let her know that she is welcome!" Mira called out. "I pray they stay with us."

"They will," Golthis said. "A wolf smells a free meal there's your new best friend. They are a thieving and murderous tribe of animals."

"They will one day more than pay their way with the tribe," Thais said.

"My father—may the gods forgive his murderous soul— would have taken a club to me knowing I allowed a wolf to share spoils of a hunt."

"We have more this hunt than any of us can eat," Thais said. "Now we leave the herd to the Ooma."

"They were polite to let us go at it first."

"They have plenty of time. We must make it home before the snows."

"Well, I have seen the Cold Days fly in brutally early," Golthis said, gazing at the endless blue skies of this prairie land.

"We should leave in the morning, even before the sun rises."

"And so we will. I admire this land for its god-sent herds of meat; but give me the mountains and no strange tribes to worry about."

Mira watched Wolf trot off to his mate. The big she-wolf, Dona, finally stood out of the grass. She was all white, like a wolf made of snow. They would make beautiful puppies, Mira prayed.

She gathered up her baby, Shana, wandered down the stream and—hidden in the rushes—washed herself. She did not like this stream, brown and muddy and sluggish, so unlike the crystal clear waters of the mountain river she had known since birth. She stared out at the horizon of green hills and thought of her mother, Adele, of old Keane the spear maker, of Haldana, holy man of the Tolai, of her twin brother and sister, Kem and Pak.

"Soon we will see you again. And then there will be a feast."

She watched the white she-wolf gobbling the meat Wolf had taken her. Mira longed to set off for home, but as always there would be a bitter sweet taste in her mouth. Another adventure would come to an end.

Mira filled a wooden bowl with water and began sponging her baby. Shana, in her soft deer skin diapers, cooed and burbled happily. Her baby had seen more adventures than Mira had ever dreamed about, and often indicated the fierce disposition of her father.

The Witch of the Conai had foretold that Shana would be a child of war; and she seemed to be fulfilling that destiny, her imp face often pouty and defiant. It did indeed seem to be a time of great change, as all the workers of magic had foretold; times of war, not only between the tribes of men but the very gods themselves. Never had Mira seen a sky battle as that storm, the gods gone mad in their fury and rage.

Mira herself had a very restless spirit; she had hunted the bison herds, and she had fought with the Four Tribes against the greatest warriors of the plains, the Menkala; she knew the scalding terror and joy of danger, and she feared it and she loved it. The madness of battle had made her feel more alive than she had ever felt. Mira, child of the wolf totem, was known to many tribes out here—the woman who hunts and fights with men, the woman with the wolf.

She smiled, knowing she was in the songs of tribes she would never know and never hear.

She dried her baby and carried Shana back up to the camp. The sun god was crawling downward behind the purple-red mountains in the distance. The Four Tribes had avoided the Lion Pass and taken a longer trail out of the mountains, avoiding trouble with the Northern Menkala. Far north was the Great Flat River. Mira had never seen it, but vowed one day to. She Had seen the impossible ones, the wooly mammoths who wandered these hills like slumberous gods. Those whose flesh was so filling and clothed in fat.

She looked for her dog, but Wolf had vanished into the tall grasses that whispered forever in this land. Shana had gone to sleep, and Mira lay her on her bison hide bed. The camps of the Four Tribes were astir, as last preparations were being made for the long and torturous trip back into the mountains. Stone tipped spears stood like pickets in the emerging moon.

She would sing of this place when the Cold Days came and the tribe gathered round the tribal fire. She would call this camp the Place of the Great Storm.

Two . . .

Far away to the east the Menkala camp lay. Regga, leader of the warriors, stood with his chieftain, Xarran, and stared eastward at the far lights of hundreds of campfires that glowed off the clouds.

The Paw-Nee.

Karas, the brother of Thais, stood with them, and they watched Carilus, the Mogan, trudge up the hill to where they stood. It was an overcast night that promised rain, and the mood of all four men was foul. Bad luck had plagued the Southern Menkala for more than two seasons: The river tribes of the west mountains had defeated them, killing many of their best warriors. Now the vast tribes of Paw-Nee were invading from the plains of the east; Northern Menkala pushed across the Flat River, and desert tribes crept in from the south to harvest the great bison herd that covered the hills. The bison attracted the tribes of men as endless grass attracts endless locust.

The men watched Mogan Carilus approach slowly up the hill. He wore a grim face, and when he reached the top of the hill he stared at the lights glowing off the clouds.

"Their campfires make a great light against the sky," he muttered, to no one but himself.

"Our scouts are watching," Xarran said. "I myself have seen their camp."

"We cannot attack them?"

"No, Mogan; they are too many."

"Do we risk meeting with them?"

"They would take it as weakness," Xarran said. "We can do no more this night than watch."

"They hunt on the lands of Menkala!"

"It has been a long time of bad signs," Regga said in a low voice.

The Mogan looked at him. "We have come a great distance to stand and watch."

"They are too many," Xarran repeated. "Their teepees cover the very earth. One Menkala can kill many Paw-Nee; but they are too many."

"What then, Regga?" Mogan said.

"We must wait and watch. If they break into smaller hunting parties, we can destroy them. But such a camp as that I have never seen. If we show patience, and the gods turn to our favor, then we can attack and destroy them."

"We have angered the gods in some way, this is true."

"We let Thais and his mountain people steal from the herd!" Karas blurted out, causing the other three men to stare at him. "When we failed to destroy the mountain tribes, the gods frowned and other tribes sensed weakness. I spoke long ago of my brother, and how he would challenge us and weaken us."

"You ache to kill your brother," said Xarran. "But the great enemy is there." He pointed to the lights of the campfires. "The Four Tribes are just that, four tribes stretched down a mountain river. They will never be a true danger to us."

"I know my brother. The gods are angry that we have failed to kill him and his people, few as they are."

"Well spoken," Regga said. "We must find a way to make the gods favor us. Ever we have been lords of our domain. Ever the other tribes have feared to even speak our name."

"We must unite with the north," said Xarran. "Together we can take back our lands and the bison. If all of the Menkala unite, we will again be lords of this land. We must stop fighting one another!"

"The gods will tell us if this can be done," Carilus said. "I will make a sacrifice to the War God and He will speak to me."

At that very moment, to his astonishment, the sky spoke to him. The God spoke to him.

Karas let out a gasp. "Look!" he said, pointing to the sky.

The men stood in awe and fear as they watched a tail of fire blaze suddenly out of the sky. None could speak beholding the fire-tail streak to the earth, trailing a robe of illuminated smoke, only three hills distant. They heard a deep booming roar.

"By the gods!" Xarran finally whispered.

"The God," Mogan Carilus said.

"What was that flame?"

"The God has sent us something. I have heard of this in Mogan songs that tell of gods sending power from the skies, power that trails fire behind it."

Xarran stared at the dark horizon. "What must we do?"

"We must go where the fire finger pointed; there over those hills."

The men set off toward the valley where the fire had struck earth. Many giant creatures stalked the night around them; dire wolves, giant prairie lions, swarms of jackals and hyenas, murderous carnivores that followed the bison herd. Beast voices echoed out of the dark: cackles and howls, growling throats, snarls and screams. But the men were Menkala, and no animal would dare challenge their spears and atlatls and torches. They climbed a last hill and smelled scorched grass.

"Down there," Regga said. "See the glow?"

It was a tiny glow of red in a ring of fire. They crept down the hill toward the strange scene. Prairie grass around it had caught fire, and the men spent several minutes putting it out. Then they knelt round the strange red light.

"What is it?" Regga whispered.

"The old songs tell of this." Carilus stared into the starry, moonless night. "It is a stone."

"A stone?"

"A stone sent from the gods; a stone of great power and magic, sent on the spear of fire. This is the sign we have been waiting for. The gods have sent this to us."

"I will take it," Karas said, wanting to prove his bravery to them. He approached the glowing ember half-buried in the turf, no larger than a man's fist. How could such a small thing make such a fire tail in the sky? It sizzled angrily; all around it the grass was roasted; ash smell blew on the wind. The Mogan looked up at the glittering black sky.

"Stay back from it," Xarran commanded. "It is growing darker. Let it cool off."

The men squatted round the glowing stone, praying with Carilus to the God who had sent it. They watched the God Stone as it grew less red and finally settled into black, like a fist of coal. At last Xarran rose and picked it up.

"Still warm."

"Let me have it," Carilus said.

The holy man held the black stone in his hand and felt its odd warmth. His eyes grew trancelike as the other men watched him. The smell of the burnt grass blew away in the wind, and now was only the quiet, ominous sky of stars.

"This was sent to give us great power," the Mogan said at last.

"The sky god favors us at last," said Xarran.

"No, this was not sent by the sky god. He speaks with the yellow spears and the roaring voice. This God Stone was sent to us by the god of war."

"What does Menka tell us?" Regga asked. "Does he favor us?"

"Yes. He favors us at last." Mogan, fondling the strange warm stone from the sky, gazed at the dark horizon, the slight glow of the Paw-Nee camp. "We must unite with the Menkala of the north. We must make war, until all tribes who challenge the Menkala are destroyed, until we are once again lords of this domain. We must destroy everything. We must proclaim to all of the Menkala, Northern and Southern, that the War God lives in this stone."

Chieftain Xarran and Karas stared at the stone. Already it disturbed them that the Mogan had taken it for his own. "The god of war is telling us that we must destroy Thais first," Karas spoke up. "We must avenge ourselves against the mountain tribes."

"I must wait for the war god to tell me more. I will eat a magic thing and He will speak to me. One thing I know . . ." The Mogan looked down at the black stone in his hand. "This is a gift of great power. This will make us masters again of the Short Hills."

Three . . .

The expedition of the Four Tribes made camp in the dry, shrub-covered foothills of the eastern mountains. Mira washed herself and her baby at a clear brook that threaded the rocky land. Jella, the mate of Golthis, squatted beside her and washed her three older children who had come along on the adventure.

Mira's eyes said goodbye once again to the Short Hills. In the distance she spotted a pride of lions padding majestically under the moon. She could smell the cool west wind blowing out of the mountains, and the beloved scent of pine. She smiled and cooed at Shana: "My little papoose, soon we will be back home at the caves, and you will see Kem and Pak and grand mama. And I'll bet your daddy will make you another doll of straw and goat down."

"Back home. Thank the gods," Jella sighed. "This land takes the life from me. How can so many giant beasts live out there? How do they survive storms like that one?"

"We have songs of adventure in our throats."

Jella shaded her hands as she gazed out from the foothills. "There's Wolf and that strange white mate of his. It looks like they plan to stay with us."

"Every evening Dona creeps in closer to the fire. I hope that soon Wolf will bring her into the camp. She will be afraid going into the high mountains."

"Look at our men strutting around those dead shagbeards. You'd think they were gods of the hunt."

"We will eat well in the Cold Days; and think of the bison furs to curl up in."

"Still, I'll cry my eyes out when we get home to the caves. I'm not one for adventure; not like you. But my children are still excited. They will brag forever to their friends. And if I leave Golthis alone too long, he'll get himself killed."

Etain, Chieftain of the Tolai, hobbled up to Golthis and Thais, who stood gazing out at the Short Hills. Etain was still nursing a leg broken under a Menkala club in the Great Mountain Battle east of the Conai village, and he would probably always limp.

"Any signs?" he asked Thais.

"No, we are alone."

"But for our new friends, the Snake Tribe." Said Golthis.

"It will be a hard trek back to the caves." Etain stared at the travois of dried bison meat that stretched down the stream. "I think we may have taken too much this time."

"You can never have too much meat," Golthis said. "Jella says that by next spring I'll be too fat to walk."

Thais smiled. "This was a great success; for us and for the Ooma. "They will probably harvest more than we have."

"They don't have mountains to climb," Golthis said.

"We should also thank the far Paw-Nee," said Etain. "Though I've never seen one."

"They look much like the Menkala," Thais said. "They are a vast empire that rules the flat plains far east of here. Ever they have been the enemy of the Menkala."

"Too many men crowd this land." Golthis had spotted the lions and he watched them padding in the distance. "I would like some day to hunt one of those creatures. One at a time, of course."

"It is a Menkala test of manhood to kill a lion without help," Thais said.

"Have you killed one of the monsters?" Etain also spotted the lions.

"Yes."

The Four Tribes had spread out along the foothills, and many women who had braved the trip were squatting along the brook washing clothes and children. Thais had not approved of allowing children on such a venture, but as his own baby daughter was along, he couldn't very well protest. This far south of the Flat River, there was little danger, especially after the peace agreement with the Ooma. In only three seasons the Four Tribes had gone from starving and isolated and in danger of destruction to a powerful force to be reckoned with. This was the power of the bison; and the power of unity.

But he of all people knew the Menkala. They had suffered many set-backs in the last few seasons; they had lost many warriors. But no other tribe of men that he knew could match the savagery and fighting skills of the people he had been born to. His own brother Karas and his former best friend Regga ruled the Menkala army; they had declared themselves his sworn enemies and vowed to the war god to parade his severed head through the Menkala camp. Such a vow was not to be taken lightly, but there was nothing for it. Thais had been raised a Menkala warrior, and in that culture only one creed ruled: Kill or Die.

"By the gods," Golthis said. "It will be fine to see the river again. Then we will throw a feast to be remembered in songs forever." He looked sidelong at Thais. "It would be better, of course, if I had one of those lion skins to wear."

"There were plenty of them shadowing the camp. I would have tried to stop you."

"Well," Etain said, gazing with satisfaction at the mountain expedition settling down to camp. "Again I'm proud of our people. The hardships of these adventures, and the bison meat, have made us strong. I only wish my son could have seen this."

Thais stared off sadly. Mira's brother, Elat, had been killed in the Mountain Battle with the Menkala. "May conas tessa, mai kagga sodra, no co entiak atta," Thais said in his native tongue. (The swift runner, the fierce warrior, the strong man—none can beat death).

That evening Thais settled into bed with Mira and Shana. Clouds formed in the south, and he thought they may have a light rain. Shana lay in her papoose, sleeping in peace; Mira snuggled up to him. They loved having pillow talk before going to sleep.

"Another adventure, My Love." Thais kissed her.

"Another adventure." Mira lay against his fierce, muscular body, took in his scent of leather and wind. "Now the hateful trip back home, this time with more loads than I could have imagined."

"The hunters have learned fast how to hunt the shagbeards. The mountains made good hunters and good warriors."

"But not as the Menkala."

"No. Not as the Menkala."

"Those monsters are far away from us, from Shana. May the distant Paw-Nee tear them from the world." Mira remembered the first time she had seen a Menkala, a scout from the raiding party that had destroyed the Palotai village and murdered her childhood friend, Adela. How their savage animal bodies were tatooed with all monsters and snakes and white skulls and demon flames. "May your first tribe be swiped from the earth," she said.

"I don't think that will happen, Mira. We defeated them, but only because we were lucky—very lucky. Tomorrow we will be back in our mountains and I will begin to relax. Look at Shana, how she snores. Maybe she dreams of her adventure."

"It could be that Turok dreams of his adventure too."

"Who is Turok?"

Mira kissed him. "Your son—I think. I believe."

Thais stared at her. "My son?"

Mira blushed. "A woman should not speak, even to her mate, about some things."

"I am not easy to shock," Thais said. "Tell me, Love."

Mira turned away, embarrassed. "I have not bled in the moon time. Jella tells me another child might be inside me."

Thais stared at her in wonder. "By the gods, Mira."

"I will speak to the Witch when we reach the Conai. I feel a strangeness in my belly. I think there might be life in me, and I think it might be a boy."

"Turok."

"If it is a boy—and if you approve the name."

"A good name." Thais smiled and kissed her. Night fell over the foothills, and they could hear the restless Short Hills in the east, the animals and night birds echoing their voices across the great emptiness. "You will carry nothing back to the caves."

"I did before."

"Not this time, My Love. You strained yourself beyond strength last time, and we were lucky; but you know what I think about luck."

"It never does last," Mira said.

In the middle of the night, the two wolves growled from the fringe of the campsite. Thais woke to a tingle on the back of his neck. He lay still, letting his eyes adjust to the dark; then slowly he picked up his atlatl and loaded an arrow into it. He sat up, making as little noise as possible. He stared into the short scrub brush that grew along the brook. He heard a hush. Presently he saw the figure ghost out of the brush and vanish into the dark.

Next morning he took Etain aside: "Tell no one; but a Menkala spy was among us last night."

Etain stared at him, then to the east. "Menkala! How do you know this?"

"I caught a glimpse of him."

"You are sure it was a Menkala?"

"Yes."

"You're lucky he didn't kill you."

"But for the wolves, he might have," Thais said. "They certainly want me dead. It probably is that Regga or my brother ordered against it. They want no one else to claim their kill."

"Our sentries didn't detect him."

"Menkala move like shadows. This spy will report our strength and where we are. They will not venture into the mountains again, I think. But now they know the route we are taking to the herds."

"Will he return?"

"I doubt it. He has a long travel back to their main camp. He found out what he needs to know; but, Chieftain, this is a bad thing."

"I will double the camp guard." Etain looked at his daughter and grand-daughter down at the brook. "What is Mira doing?"

She was squatting, holding a chunk of meat out at the brush along the stream. She had to keep pushing Wolf away from it. Thais smiled.

"She is making a friend. Watch."

Presently the white she-wolf, Dona, crept out of the brush and belly-crawled up to Mira. Mira was whispering softly to her. Dona crept up to her, snatched the meat from her hand and vanished back into the cover.

"By the gods," Etain marveled. "My daughter always had a way with those creatures."

Four . . .

The Paw-Nee hunting party camped for the night, spreading their bison robes out on the bare prairie hill. The low roar of the great bison herd made a background that was ignored. Sentries saw wolves slinking just beyond the camp, circling round, smelling the fresh kill of the day. The hunters were used to such beasts, and hyenas, lions, even wolverines staying close to the party and its piles of food.

In this place at this time, creatures far larger and faster and more savage than any man were common. One man could not hope to fight one dire wolf; and ten men could not best one of the giant lions. But these big wolves that crept round the camp would not dare attack. The hunters had atlatls and long spears of wood and flint. And the men had fire, the savage magic that every creature feared.

Only these wolves did not fear fire—because they were not wolves. A sleepy guard stiffened as one of the wolves shot out of the dark—a Menkala warrior in wolfskin—and ripped more than half his head off with a flint dagger. Trained from birth to be able to leap out of nowhere and kill quickly and silently, the Menkala disposed of the camp guards. Then, throwing off their wolf skins, revealing muscled bodies tattooed with serpents, monsters, skulls, all things cruel and savage, they fell upon the sleeping Paw-Nee. Regga, leader of the warriors, was learning from the traitor Thais, and attacking men in sleep at night. His men had grumbled, but murder is murder, and they made a bloody mess of human gristle and human bone. It was not war or battle; it was the quick and efficient butchering of men.

Very soon it was over, and Regga was pleased that it had gone so quietly. It was contrary to the Menkala way, he knew, to cheat the warriors out of the sounds of their victims, the cries and begging and screams they worshipped. But Regga had grown up with Thais, and he knew enough to adapt the strategies of his childhood companion. They had been best friends, in the days when Thais was a Menkala. Regga knew that he was a good leader—better than the late Tan Mok, the legend. He knew that he could come to rule the Menkala; his plans were already maturing to that end. He knew that he was no Thais.

The hunting party of 28 Paw-Nee lay dead on the plains. The Menkala warriors, led by Regga, paraded among the dead, cutting off gushing heads with razor flint knives and taking souvenirs. Others began preparing a fire. It was a strange nightmare under the half-moon. The blood-gut smells flowed on the wind, attracting hyenas, lions and all forms of night scavengers. Those creatures of violence and night, those things formed by nature to kill. At last here was the awful triumph of the Menkala.

"Quiet! No fire," Regga said to his men, causing them to stare. He looked to the northeast, where over 500 Paw-Nee hunters camped. "Smoke will bring notice."

"It is the Menkala way," Karas said. "And to stave the skulls."

"No time for that," Regga said. "And from now on we waste no spears on staving dead skulls."

"It is the way. Our men will not understand. They will believe we are angering the war god."

"The war god has sent us the stone. Menka lives in the stone. His power is with us again. He commands that we must change our ways. We were lucky to find these. But over those hills they are too many, and they know it."

"As you wish," Karas said, but was unsure.

"Let them cut off the heads, but no staving and no fires—this time. They have saved the hunting party leader for you. Cut off his head and let's be gone. The message will be clear enough."

"I will cut it off slow," Karas said. "That is the way. A slice and then wait; then another slice. They will see how he suffered."

"No, Karas, do it quick. We don't need to alert them to one of their own screaming in the night."

Karas stared at the ground. "I will thank my fortune anyway. We were lucky to have come upon these hunters."

"No, it is not luck; it is because of the God Stone that these Paw-Nee lay dead before us. It is as it used to be, that the Menkala rule this world. We of all have the God Stone."

Karas nodded, but was concerned. "We have such power from the war god," he said. "Can we now attack and destroy the mountain tribes? I ask only to cut off the head of my brother and restore the family honor. There will be no danger then, if I make it slow and terrible."

"Soon," Regga said. "And for me, the Giant of the South, who they say killed Tan Mok. I hear the warriors speak of Tan Mok. He is mightier in death than he was in life. They say when they think I am not listening that I am no Tan Mok. Only by killing the man who killed Tan Mok will I gain respect. So remember: Golthis the Giant is mine."

"And Thais is mine. And the family he has made that mocks the gods. They are mine."

A day later they reported the victory to the Chieftain and the Mogan in the main camp.

"At last we have struck our enemies," Xarran said. "But the men say you showed little cruelty, Regga."

"The camp of the Paw-Nee was very close. We would have attracted them with screams and torture. We had no time."

"It is ever our way to compete for cruelty."

"A party of Paw-Nee killed," said Mogan Carilus. "It is a sign that the God Stone is returning power to us."

Regga bowed to the holy man, knowing that after his defeat in the mountains Xarran had no faith in him; that the Mogan still did, and that was the only reason he still lived. "Well said, Mogan," he whispered.

Five . . .

The great celebration at the home of the Conai was building up to a fever of savage joy. The great bonfire roared, the Four Tribes danced and sang and feasted, each painted in the colored animals of the mountains: mocking bird, mountain sparrow, snowy cottontail, wise owl, fierce hawk.

Mira, her face painted in silver streaks of the wolf, danced the fertility dance with other women who were either plainly pregnant, or suspected to be. The great bonfire blazed skyward into the black, moon-cut night. Smoke billowed over the mountains. The tribe, happy over their bowls of rich bison stew, chanted and encouraged the women dancers.

When the drums echoed away, Mira sat once again next to Thais, painted as he always was, as the brown and tawn saber tooth. Shana, painted rust and white, as a baby fox, slept in her papoose. Wolf was away in the trees with his mate. The white wolf slept ever closer to the humans, and Mira had even managed to pet her. Dona was getting used to Mira's soft voice and gifts of chew bones.

The white she-wolf, Dona, would sit on a rise and stare, sitting like a statue, at the new world she was entering.

Sometimes she would raise her white face to the sky and howl, wolf howling with her.

I know, Mira thought. You are finding a new adventure, girl-wolf. And you are afraid.

Etain, painted as a wise black bear, came up to her and bent himself to her ear.

"My daughter," he whispered. "The witch wants to speak to you."

Mira felt a chill. She looked around the savage bonfire celebration. "Where is she?"

"Golthis says her cave is there, away from the others. He said that you would find it by following the smell of incense. He has never gone up there; no one goes up there but the shamen. The witch does not attend the gatherings of the tribes."

Mira stood. She looked up at the dark caves in the boulders along the river.

"Daughter," Etain said. "Golthis tells me that you should not speak of what you see in the cave of the witch."

"I will find her cave." Mira turned, bent down and kissed Thais, who had listened. "It will be fine. I do not fear Zianna."

Thais kissed her back, smudging her wolf face. "It may be that Zianna fears you."

Mira left the celebration and climbed up to the caves of the Conai, wandering over rocks and boulders. Presently she smelled a sweet cedar smoke. The cave of the witch was only a dark crevice in the boulders, many strides away from the main tribal caves. The sweet shrubs, those that grew in the dry places of the mountains, those with the incense leaves and prickly scent, almost smothered the cave entrance. Mira approached, and when she was at the narrow doorway, the voice of the witch said, "Enter, young one."

Mira crawled into darkness faintly lit by a small fire. She could only see the witch's creamy eyes beyond the glow; the rest of Zianna was lost in the shadows. Mira lowered herself to the dark cave floor, onto a rug of bobcat. Outside, the loud celebration echoed in the night. Zianna's eyes studied her, and Mira let her own eyes find the gloom.

The cave of the witch was too dark to see any adornment; there was only the small fire and sweet, strange smells.

She waited for Zianna to speak, but the witch merely transferred her eyes to the fire, as if something were written there.

Finally the silence got the best of Mira: "I believe I have another child in me," she blurted out.

"No matter that," said the witch. "If so, it is little bigger than a pinion nut."

"Why do you never join the feasts?"

The question seemed to startle Zianna. She stared into the fire, her eyes fatal, mesmerized. "I am never at the feasts. I have nothing to celebrate. My presence ruins feasts. No matter; the bison flesh makes the river tribes strong and warm."

"Never have I tasted such wonderful meat."

"I can no longer eat it; my teeth are all gone. One must have teeth to eat bison."

They were silent for some moments. Finally Mira asked, "Why do you want to speak to me?"

The eyes of the witch blinked up from the fire to Mira's face. "You are the only one besides the shamen who have ever entered this domain."

"I am honored," Mira said.

"All else fear to even look at my home. But you do not have much fear, young one; and your mate even less. I summoned you here because you have brought a great power and a great magic from the east."

"What?"

"The white wolf."

Mira was puzzled. "Dona?"

"It is more than a dona; it is a Hosho Dona. Your Menkala boy knows of this. The fiercest Menkala will not dare approach you if you are with the Hosho Dona."

"She is the mate of my wolf."

Zianna stared away, working her gums. Mira knew that the witch had spent much of her childhood as a captive in the tribes of the northern Menkala.

"When you return to your Tolai caves, you must speak to Haldana of this white wolf. He will paint the Hosho Dona onto the wall of his cave. Then he will eat a magic thing and go into the realm of the gods. Maybe he can find out what this means."

As her eyes adjusted to this cedar smelling darkness, Mira could make out shadow rags hanging along the rock walls. She could not imagine what they were.

"How can I know what the gods want?" she asked.

"You can never know for certain. But you are becoming known as the Wolf Girl. And now the gods send to you a Hosho Dona."

They were both silent for some time. Mira felt sorry for Zianna, so lonely her life seemed to be; the ugliest of women, tolerated only because everyone feared her. Great power, great loneliness. Mira hoped she was relieving some of the loneliness.

At last the witch seemed to read her thoughts. Her face grew soft: "If the gods favor us, we all may find our destinies. I have found mine."

"I'm afraid of my destiny," Mira said. "What I must do to please the gods."

Zianna tossed a powder into her solitary fire, as Shaman Haldana would do, and behind a crazy spittle of red light Mira saw her ancient, tortured face.

"Your fierce Menkala boy, your mate, does not believe the gods exist."

Mira was shocked. "How do you know this?"

"He told me. And he told you. But I would not tell others this. He has become like a god himself to the river tribes."

"He prays when the tribe prays; he gives homage, and speaks of the gods."

"I have met some like him. They are rare. There may be many others who hide their doubt and just pretend to believe."

"We do not speak of it often." Mira stared into the fire, which had returned to a quiet flame of yellow. Zianna sprinkled slivers of cedar wood onto it.

"How can the gods not be?" Mira asked.

"I only know that, belief or not, the gods have favored your mate—so far."

"I cannot understand how one could not believe in the gods."

"Your boy is Menkala. They are not easy to understand."

29

This was the dark and forbidden cave of the Witch of Conai. Mira had seen the mighty Golthis shudder glancing up at it. But she felt unexplainably at ease, even comfortable in this place of loneliness and dark magic. She longed to know, to understand the power of the witch.

"My mate is very wise. How can anyone so wise dare to believe that the gods don't exist? I can't understand this."

In the cedar glow of the flame, the witch smiled at her. "Most would be killed to admit such a thing to tribe ears," she said. "Of course Menkala are very hard to kill."

"I killed two," Mira said.

The witch's smile turned surprisingly gentle. "Mira, of the wolf totem. Born into the new world of war, of tribes in great wars. I am close to death, and you are close to life."

"I have terrible dreams of the wars between men."

"So do I, Young One."

"I am afraid for Shana! I am afraid for my children. When will this terrible madness end?"

The witch looked into her fire. "It will never end. Now you go back to the feast, your wolf face is streaking." Zianna laughed. Then, studying Mira, her eyes narrowed. "Your face is easy to read. You have a question."

"Yes," Mira said. "You have great magic powers. Everyone knows you have great powers. I would like to know . . ."

"Know what, Mira?" the witch said after a pause.

"I would like to know what power is, what magic truly is. I have seen the magic of Shaman Haldana, and I have seen your magic. I have seen the impossible magic of the gods—things I never could believe—the fire songs come to life. I am here in your domain. I have brought the white wolf to the river people. Please tell me what magic is; what power is."

The witch hesitated. Zianna seemed to be communicating with the fire set before her in a ring of stones. The feast echoed beyond in the river valley. Mira tried to identify the shadows that hung just in the darkness.

Finally Zianna let out a long sigh. "Power and magic— the same thing," she said. "They look different, maybe— they seem different. They are one thing."

"I don't understand."

"It is simple, Mira: power is belief. Magic is belief. I have killed warriors with my look and my spells—great strong men that I made grow sick and die like worms—only because I Told them they would die like worms, and only because they beLieved they would die like worms." Zianna cackled out a laugh that made Mira jump back. "I made them die because I saw and I took the great power: Belief."

"Belief," Mira said.

"I am old and facing death," the witch said. "You are young and facing life. Belief is everything, whether it is true or not. That is what magic is."

"She is very lonely, My Love," Mira said. "Zianna is very sad."

"Yes, I know."

"I cry for her."

"She has had a rough life."

Mira burrowed into Thais and kissed his bare chest. "She spoke to me of Dona—Wolf's white mate."

The Tolai had camped mid-way between lands where the river curved upward toward home. Mira felt the bitter sweet joy of returning home.

"The white wolf."

"Why would she speak to me of this?"

"The Menkala believe the white wolf is sacred. That it has magic."

"They all believe that."

"Yes. They believe that."

"And you were raised to believe that."

"Yes."

Mira looked at her mate. "But you do not believe."

"No, Mira. I do not believe that the color of a wolf is sacred."

The white wolf lay with Mira's wolf just beyond the fringe of campfire. Dona was adjusting to life with humans, and Mira could stroke and groom her, as she did Wolf. Thais was fairly sure that a wolf from the plains would easily adapt to the mountains.

"When did you speak to the witch?" Mira asked.

Thais looked at her. "I've spoken to Zianna many times."

"About what?"

Thais put his arm round her and tickled her ribs. "Mira, who always needs to Know."

She giggled against him. "Tell me!" she commanded.

"We spoke of the Menkala often; and the changing of the world."

Mira felt her stomach roll. "Do you believe the world is changing?"

"It seems so. While we were away on this trek, some of the older hunters came across a strange tribe of the north.

They had to speak with the hands; but these men told of the great ice growing in the north."

"It is in the old Tolai songs, of the great ice in the north. Do you believe in it?"

Thais shrugged. "I have never seen it. The far northern Crow tribe claims that some of their hunters have seen it; mountains taller than ours, only made of ice. A place where it is always the Cold Days."

Mira stared darkly into their campfire. She had not believed that there could be a land of no mountains; yet she had seen them. Could there be a land of pure ice—and what could live there?

"Also we spoke of you a few times," Thais said. "Zianna believes you will play a great part in the story of our times."

"I don't understand how."

Thais studied the fire. "I do not believe in visions of the future. I have always believed that the future cannot be told because it is not yet real. But I agree with the witch that the times of people are in change. And I sense that the very earth herself is changing. The ways we have always known must, some of them, be abandoned. Kat el si."

"What does that mean?"

"So be it." Thais looked down at his daughter, asleep bundled in her papoose. "We spoke of this one also. Shana, Child of War."

"I pray it is not so." Mira stared away at the familiar mountains, the beloved river she had known since birth. Wolves began howling far away across the river valley, and she saw a white form—Dona—rise up to stare. At last the moon climbed over the mountain peaks, and she could see the speckles of light on the river. She did not want the world to change; but as her mother always told her, the world changes with every beat of the heart. Only three seasons ago Mira had been a girl on the cusp of womanhood. Now she was a mother. She had made several treks to the Short Hills; she had killed bison with the hunters; she had gone into battle and killed the savage Menkala; she was in distant songs sung across distant campfires.

She was thankful when they approached the home caves of the Tolai; yet she was also sad that the world would again become the safe and tedious daily business of survival and work. She knew that soon, when her exhaustion had worn off, she would cast her eyes to the east. She longed for female companionship; but her best friend Adela had been murdered by the Menkala long ago. Mira had hoped to befriend her brother's mate-to-be, but Elat too had been killed by the Menkala. And Jella was far down the river in the Conai tribe.

Shana was taking her first steps, doll-walking like a new born fawn. She was beginning to gurgle out sounds that would soon be words. Far to the east great armies of warriors battled for the bison; here was the ageless sound of the river and the quiet peace of the mountains. Mira fingered her ivory necklace totem from the tooth of a mammoth. Thais had given it to her seasons ago, and she would touch it when she spoke to the gods. Now the moon bathed the river valley. Shana slept peacefully. Thais rested, but she knew that if she were to speak he would come instantly awake. He explained to her that the tribe who raised him would train boys from an early age how to rest muscles and mind; but to only lay at the rim of sleep, so that they could come instantly awake and be ready for action in a heartbeat. Mira had witnessed it in the Great Mountain battle east of the Conai.

She didn't speak. She was very worn out, but not sleepy. She stared into the shadow boulders that formed crazy giant stairs into the darkness of the mountain. She couldn't see Wolf or Dona. All round the party of the Tolai hunters slept beside the sacred river. Piles of dried bison meat, covered in their own hides, lay on the travois. Heaps of treasure from the gods.

Thais had said that the gods of the Short Hills were not the gods of the mountains. Everything seemed larger out there; the beasts were so great, the horizon beyond any eyes. The sky was spectacular at night, revealing light gods of the sky Mira had never seen before. She remembered the smells—of sweet grass wind, the rank odor of the bison herd, so powerful it made the very air. She remembered lying on the soft grass of that strange land and listening to the night birds. She thought of the long-snouts, the mammoth herd, and how it had seemed so like boulders moving across the plains. She had climbed one of the dying monsters, and helped to spear it dead. So much she had done that Mira could not in her girlhood have ever imagined. Mira remembered it all, and she shivered.

She remembered the Witch of the Conai.

Six . . .

Mira's mother Odele entered her cave space. She wore a gentle, but sad smile.

Mira was working an intricate coil of hemp that would make a rope. She smiled at her mother, but she knew that something was wrong.

"I saw Keane enter Father's cave," she said. "What is it, Mama?"

Odele sat and suddenly stroked her daughter's long, brown hair. All the tribe knew that when Keane was called upon to a private place, something was wrong.

"I will be leaving you soon, Mira," Odele said. "I will be leaving you all soon."

"What? Why was Keane up here?"

"I wanted him to look at a growth in my breast."

Mira was scared. "What does that mean?"

"You've seen it—but only a few times: the growth that will appear on women my age. A mark of pride to some, for it's said that it means your soul is so strong the god who takes the soul has to encage it." Odele stared off. "Look after your father. Look after Kem and Pak—look after Shana and the one who lives in you."

"Mama, you can't be saying this. Did Keane tell you this? He can be wrong."

"He's not wrong. He only told me what I already knew. I am dying, daughter—and I think quick. I felt it some time ago; and the gods have spoken to me in my dreams. Keane agreed that it will happen very soon. This inside my body is making me very weak and weary. I move in pain."

"No!" Mira stared at her in terror. They said nothing for some time; then Mira's face wrinkled in sorrow and rage. "No, Mama, I can't lose you. It's not fair of the gods."

"Never say things like that about the gods. It is fair. I have seen half of my children survive. I have seen my son die brave in battle. I have seen my little matchlings survive the cold days. And I have seen you survive all your early sickness to become a great woman. I cannot tell you how proud I am of you, My Papoose."

"No." Mira cried against her mother. "We'll cut in and take out the growth."

"That would only kill me the quicker."

"Keane could do it."

"No, he cannot. It comes to all of us, Mira."

"I can't lose you."

"You will never lose me."

Mira lay against her mother as she had when she was a sick child, fighting for life. Odele stroked her hair. "Life was a good dream, My Papoose. Now at last I will be with the gods."

Mira began sobbing uncontrollably. "No, Mama! Please don't die! Please don't leave me, Mama!"

"You will have to be strong for the family. And you are strong, of all I've ever seen. I will be watching you from the land beyond, and I will be smiling. Don't cry, My Little Papoose. You have made my life a joy."

Thais approached the cave space of Keane, made the grunt of notice; slid the old man's deer hide door open just a crack, the Tolai respect for privacy.

"Enter?" he asked.

"Oh, Thais—good. Yes, enter."

Keane was as highly respected as the Shaman and Chieftain Etain, but his cave was smaller, and adorned with nothing but tools and weapons, the ones he had crafted in his seasons that—Thais guessed by looking at them—were so good the old man couldn't part with them. Otherwise, only a fire pit, some hide rugs and a few bowls and spits.

Hanging from the rock walls on straps of rawhide were atlatls and their arrows, spears, knives, hammer stones, awls, hatchets better than even that of Golthis, Giant of the South. In the dim firelight, beautiful blades of flint glittered like jewels.

Keane grunted. "I know what you're thinking. Maybe you can have a few—after I'm dead."

Thais smiled. "They are all magnificent."

"They are the family I've created in my seasons. My mate, Chondra, died long ago trying to give birth to our first child. I could not bring myself to take another mate . . . I don't know why. Now these are the only children I will leave behind."

Thais sat down cross-legged on an elk rug. He couldn't stop studying the great tools and weapons. "One day we may need your children. The children of Chondra."

Keane looked at him. "They are not good at keeping an old man from loneliness; but I have plenty of young ones to teach each day. A few will master pine and sinew and resin and stone and tools. You didn't come here to talk of my trade."

"Odele," Thais said. "You are sure."

Keane looked into his fire, frowning. "I am sure."

"Mira is very sad. She cannot accept it."

"Yes, Mira. She may replace Odele as the Herb Maker."

"What?"

"She who gathers the magic things, the healing herbs and roots and barks. You didn't think Haldana—or old Keane—at our ages would be climbing into the mountains for them. Mira, as you know, is very good at it. Her mother taught her well."

"How long will it be?"

"Not long. Not long at all. Odele is already seeing the other side. Etain does not know, but she told me she went to Shaman Haldana with a dream of the other side. It was a dream of Mira and the white wolf."

"Hosho Dona," Thais said.

"But there is more. There were Menkala in the dream. Odele woke sensing a terrible danger, but not for herself. This is important, because when a soul is between the living and the dead, they can in their dreams see what will happen beyond them. Haldana was disturbed. He said that after the ceremony—after Odele passes beyond—he will travel downriver to the Conai to speak to Shaman Shandana and the Witch. We sense it; we all sense it—and so do you."

Thais stared into the fire. "Yes."

"I know you worry about Mira. But she is too much in love with life to let death defeat her. She has always been a fierce one."

"I have noticed that."

Keane was silent for a while, and Thais respected his silence. He stared at the weapons on Keane's wall. He thought of the Menkala.

As if reading his thoughts, Keane said, "The people of your youth worship death, do they not."

"Yes."

"That is beyond my understanding. If so, why do they not just kill themselves, and achieve death?"

"Sadly, it does not work that way."

Now Keane looked at his prize weapons, a lattice of great skill. He looked at Thais. "There will never again come a time of peace, will there?"

"I do not know," Thais said. "But I think not."

The long precession of Tolai wound up East Mountain toward the Cave of Skeletons.

At the border of the White Ring they all halted, forming an arc round the sacred ground. Many faces in the tribe—most of the young ones—were fearful. Beyond the white stones was the place where the souls of the dead rose skyward to the gods, and were never seen on earth again.

Haldana gave the Prayer of Passing, and the tribe moaned a song that was beyond any memory. Thais and Keane had carefully inspected the Travois of Honor that the holy man would transport across the forbidden white stones while the tribe chanted the Prayer of Farewell. The travois was garlanded with mountain flowers that Mira knew were her mother's favorites. Odele's body was covered in a bison blanket—a spotted one, her favorite—that Mira had made to glisten.

Shaman Haldana slid the rawhide straps of the travois onto his ancient shoulders. As the tribe bowed their heads and did not watch, the holy man drew Odele's body across the white stones and up to the Cave of Skeletons. Thais risked a look.

The old man is stronger than he looks, he thought. All in this tribe are stronger than they look.

Mira was bawling herself sick, and Thais ushered her down away from the ceremony. Looking behind him, he saw most in the tribe weeping, and it intrigued him. It was a dire crime in the tribe that had raised him. No Menkala boy dared cry after his time of the fifth season. It would have been unthinkable for a Menkala to cry at the Yala Zenda (ceremony of the dead). It would have been a show of disrespect.

Yet these people—my people—cry.

Seven . . .

Cariolus, the Mogan of the Southern Menkala, stood at the base of the holiest shrine of the plains, the Great Spire, a strange formation of sandstone that ages ago had burst out of the grass earth to point its spire at the heavens. Not far away was the Flat River, the border that separated the lands of the south Menkala from their equally savage cousins to the north.

But in these days both tribes were at war with others: the great desert tribes in the south; the endless Paw-Nee, who poured in from the flat plains of the east; the mountain tribes of the west; many, many others coming in from the north, all lured to the great bison herd that blackened the plains.

Spread out before Mogan Cariolus were hundreds of Menkala, north and south, drawn together here in this holiest place. A great magic was sweeping across the plains with incredible speed. The greatest god, the war god Menka had sent to the Menkala a stone from the sky that had trailed fire. A power for all the Menkala. A stone that bore the living power and magic of Menka, the greatest God, to whom all other gods now bowed. In these days of danger the

Menkala were ripe for a new belief, one that might return them to glory.

"MENKALA!" Cariolus yelled out over the plains, his voice echoed by others to the Menkala too far away to hear. "Menka has sent us His great power—His great magic! He has sent this not to the South Menkala, but to All Menkala! He has sent this because He favors us!

"I saw with my eyes the God Stone fly down in spear fire. Others saw; and when we touched it, it burned hotter than any fire!"

The great gathering of Menkala were all silent, enraptured. Only the far-off sound of the bison.

"Menka has sent us this magic so that we unite and, as it was in the old times, destroy our enemies and again rule our lands!"

A cheer erupted that grew into a wild roar, conquering the night, startling the very air. Fists and spears rose out of the sea of warriors; women screeched like jays.

Cariolus called for quiet, and quiet rippled toward the horizon. No tribe could view this gathering without fearing its terrible power. The death of Chieftain Xarran had made Regga the new chieftain of the Southern Menkala. He looked over at the Mogan, at the man's dazzled eyes, the hold he had over so many hundreds spread out before him. Does the Mogan think he is Menka? Does he want to become ruler of all of the Menkala?

"Menka tells us that we have become weak!" Cariolus yelled out. "That our warriors no longer show cruelty! That we are weak against the Paw-Nee and the Ooma! That we fight ourselves! Menka has sent us great power and great

James Howerton

magic—and a great message: that with the God Stone in our hands we can destroy all of our enemies—that the time of the Menkala has come!"

Again a roar echoed loud against the Great Spire. Regga looked out over the gathering; never had he imagined such a host, all cheering one man. Xarran had wanted Regga dead; they both craved such power. Xarran, who ate too many river berries and died suddenly. The Mogan eats this power, Regga thought. As the Snake People eat the magic of the cactus.

"We gather here—my brothers—to unite as one people under the God Stone! To destroy those who would invade our lands and take the buffalo!"

Cheers, roars, the world changing. Rising of a savage empire, a demon mass gathered before the God Stone of Menka. Regga watched the Mogan. He was no longer shocked at the sight of so many people. He wondered at the Mogan's eagerness to take the God Stone when first they had found it, to instantly make it his. If it belongs to all the Menkala, then it does not belong to one.

"Behold the God Stone!" Cariolus roared out. He held the blackened stone high in the air, and the hundreds of gathered chanted the song of war, of death.

"Here, at the Great Spear, we will build a stone place. There the God Stone shall live, and all will approach it and pray to it!"

(The Mogan eats as all must eat, Regga thought).

A new energy, an overwhelming spirit electrified the Menkala, and they roared insanely into the clear prairie sky and begged Menka to unleash them into the world with this new magic. The most powerful god had given to them His most powerful magic:

A religion was born.

Eight . . .

How the man made it through the mountain passes, no one knew.

But the Ooma spy that Thais had met and befriended three full seasons ago appeared in the Tolai camp barely alive. The Tolai cared for him and gave him much needed sustenance. Two days later, when he was able to sign, he spoke with his hands: *I come with news.*

Thais had sent a courier to summon Golthis. He arrived with Jella and their children, who went with Shana, Kem and Pak to play at the river. Mira and Jella prepared a meal. Thais, Golthis and Etain met with the Ooma in Etain's cave.

The scout stared respectfully at Golthis: *The Giant of the South*, he signed.

"He is the same snake man we met a few seasons ago." Golthis, unable to sign, nodded at the man. "Ask him his name."

"His name is Malek-So-Conyo," Etain said.

"They give out windy names. How did he get here through the passes? My scouts tell me they are all filled with snow."

"That I want to find out," Thais said. "He wanders far; and he brings us dark news: Menkala destroyed an Ooma hunting party not far from the south trail."

Golthis traded thoughtful looks with Etain. "Then we will have to find another way to the herd. So all of his party were killed? All but him."

Thais asked with the hands, and the scout replied.

"No. He says they took some as slaves," Thais said. "Those who know how to build with wood and stone and clay. They want to build a temple for the stone."

"My scouts have heard of the stone," Golthis said. "Word is spreading fast, of a stone from the sky."

Thais frowned. The Menkala lived in portable tee-pees. He had never heard of them building permanent structures. "The God Stone has changed our enemies."

Golthis shrugged. "What is it to us that the Menkala start a new religion and build a temple of stone? It will keep them occupied."

"I'm not sure," Thais said.

"We have the white wolf," Etain said. "The witch told Mira that it's powerful magic."

"And we've beaten the Menkala twice." Golthis studied the Ooma scout with his one good eye. "If the desert snake people join with us it will make a very great force."

Thais signed, but Malek-So-Conyo grimly shook his head and signed back: *I think not; maybe in seasons to come. But now the whole Menkala nation has united, and they are raging across the Short Hills. Even the Paw-Nee are backing away, into the flat lands. In seasons to come we may venture back to the buffalo herd; but not this season.*

"It is true," Thais said. "We will have to stay in the mountains this season. We have meat to survive."

"It will be hard to keep our hunters away from the shagbeard," Etain said. "They have seen the endless food, and how easy it is to get."

"The Conai will fight for the treasures they have reaped from the Short Hills," Golthis stated. "They do not fear the Menkala; they fear seeing their children starve. They have stood up against those warriors. They have pride, Thais! How can I take that from them?"

"We defeated the Menkala in the mountains. If they were to catch us on the plains, it would not matter how strong our force. We can form a great army with the Ooma—we must. But now it is time to wait. The Menkala believe that we will go to the herd this spring—that is what they want. If we are to survive this, we must not give them what they want."

"It will not be easy keeping my hunters away from the buffalo; when they saw that herd, they were bewitched."

"Your hunters will not be able to feed the tribe if they are dead. The Ooma lost a large hunting party to the Menkala, thinking they would never venture so far south, almost to the desert lands. They did." Thais gazed out of Etain's cave and saw Shana down by the river petting the big white she-wolf. He smiled wistfully. Dona had adopted Shana and rarely left her side. Dona's body was plainly pregnant; she would pup soon, and there would be many puppies for Shana to play with and care for.

The scout, Malek-So-Conyo signed: *My people will honor the treaty with the mountain tribes, and when time has passed we will join in war with the Menkala. But our gods tell us that this is not the time.*

Thais agreed: *They are now inflamed with signs from Menka. Now they beg us to challenge them. That will change, probably. In time they will quarrel and fight themselves. The Paw-Nee will return to hunt the herd, and then the tribes of the far cold north will move again into the Short Hills. But for now, it is wise to wait. We do not give them what they want.*

Etain read the hand signs; then stared darkly out of his cave. He missed Odele, his only mate. He missed her calmness and her wisdom. He saw Mira down near the river, waddling pregnant next to Jella, their children dancing around them, showing them pebbles scooped from the sacred river. Keane, Haldana, the chieftains of the mountains, all foretold the changing of the world. He missed Odele; he missed the way the world was.

"If we do not fight," he said. "At least we should prepare."

"Yes," Thais replied. "We must prepare."

"Then it will be a lean year," Golthis said. "For us and the snake people."

"But will the Menkala again invade our mountains?"

"That worries me," Thais said. "A great change is on the wind. Our enemies might not be so easy to read. All we can do now is prepare and stay prepared." He looked at Malek-So-Conyo: *How did you reach us? How did you reach us through the high snows?*

There are secret passes in the far south mountains. You follow this river; it is the same river that waters my people. The mountains are smaller and dry. It is a long and tired journey. You should not let the Wolf-Girl take your child on this journey.

Thais frowned. *I cannot control my mate.*

Malek-So-Conyo grinned. *My mate is like that. But you risk Shana on this trip.*

I was raised to risk. And the Wolf-Girl rules me.

I will watch out for you, my river friends, the scout signed. *May we meet again at the great buffalo herd. But now the Menkala raise the God Stone. All must bow and worship this God Stone, or face death. It is told to us, of the desert, that we can no longer worship the old gods. We will die before we abandon our gods.*

We will see, in the changing of the world, what changes will be.

Nine . . .

Mira wandered up East Mountain, Wolf following in her wake. She was looking for a very elusive root, of the star plant. This would put Shaman Haldana far into the world of gods. Her apprentices, young girls of the tribe who would learn the magic things, wandered the mountain around her. Mira was the Mistress of the Earth. She had great prestige and a great song that echoed far beyond the mountains. She was heavy with a child—Turok—a boy, she believed. She had lost her mother, but she had much to be thankful for.

This was when the gods struck. Mira had a strange, painful cramp, and felt that she had to relieve herself. She found a hidden clump of bushes and squatted down. But something was very wrong. She groaned at a terrible stomach ache, and her mind clouded. Her body suddenly contorted, and she cried out. She panicked, knowing that she was giving birth and that it was too soon.

"No!" she screamed, causing the young apprentices to look up and come to her assistance.

The child spilled out of her, and Mira bent over and vomited. Horror flooded her; disbelief. She could not look at the placenta, the still-born baby that lay on the dry mountain earth. Her mind swam and she passed out.

The apprentice girls carried her to the caves, where Keane examined her. It was not life-threatening; many women lost children in birth; but this was Mira. He obtained a sleep potion from Shaman Haldana and administered it. When Mira was fast asleep, he met with Thais.

"I have seen it many times," Keane said. "The child just came too soon. No one is to blame. Mira's mother herself had two who came too soon. It is the way of things."

"It has been a very bad season for Mira," Thais said. "To have lost Odele; now to have lost Turok."

"Turok."

"That was the name she gave to him."

"It could have been another girl."

Thais sighed. His face was worn. His eyes were red. "Somehow she thought it would be a boy."

Keane studied his weapons on the wall. "I grow old and weary. I've taught many tool makers who can take over as master. Some days I yearn to be with the gods."

"Some days we all do," Thais said.

"You will have to remain strong; for Mira and for that little one. I love how Shana smiles at me and grabs my finger. I love the way she bellows at me and makes tears."

"She does that to me."

Keane had made a toy for Shana, a wooden ball. The child was nearby playing with it, giggling and grinning at her father. Wolf and his white mate were up at the entrance to Mira and Thais' cave space, where Mira mourned the death of their child. A week before, Golthis and a group of Conai hunters had accompanied Jella upriver to pay respects; Jella had miscarried once, and she was a great comfort to Mira.

But the Conai friends had returned to their homes, and now it was the sad grey skies of the Cold Days.

It was slow in coming this season, and only the highest peaks held snow. The wind was dry and cold out of the north, where it was said the great world of ice was growing. There would be no bison hunting this warm season, and the Four Tribes of the river bemoaned the loss of such treasure.

At last Mira appeared at the cave door, wandered down and up the path to the tree where Keane taught his apprentices. Wolf and pregnant Dona followed her. Mira hugged Thais and knelt down to hug Shana.

"Toy, Mama!" Shana held up her wood ball and smiled.

"Oh, yes, how pretty! Did Keane make it for you?"

"Keane made."

The old spear maker smiled. "How are you, Mira?"

"Better. I think I am done crying." Mira looked into the cold wind. "How strange this season, so far. How bright the sun and no clouds in the sky."

"Each day brings us closer to the warm days," Thais said.

"And then we go to visit the Ooma."

Thais traded looks with the spear maker: "It is a long journey, Mira. You should—"

"Shana, my pretty one; you want to see the far desert, do you not?"

"Yes, Mama."

"And to see the strange things living there and growing there. And what you will have to tell Keane when we return!"

Keane shook his head. "You make me old before my time, Mira. There are many who would look after Shana while you're gone."

"No," Mira said. "Shana will see new lands, with me and with my mate." She smiled at Thais. "I wish your son had lived—I wish Turok had lived; but he did not. I want to take our Shana into new worlds. Wolf will be with us. I think Dona will not want him around while she is weaning her pups."

"You have thought this new adventure out." Thais smiled.

"Neera, my cousin's mate, said that she would be honored to care for Dona and the pups."

"And when we return from the desert, Shana will have wolf pups to play with."

Mira smiled at Keane. "You were there when I was born."

"And you have vexed me since." Keane smiled back. "And you have made me very proud."

Ten . . .

Now Mogan Carilus was dead, Regga proclaimed the new Mogan of the South Menkala, and Karas the new chieftain. Regga soon began performing human sacrifices:

The woman who had questioned the God Stone was tied down on her knees. She knelt before the tall spire of limestone that shaded the half-completed temple of the new god. She had been a strong and out-spoken woman; now she whimpered and shivered in her misery. She did not understand why this was happening to her.

"The women of the Paw-Nee are given power!" Regga called out to the gathered masses. "The women of the Mountains are allowed power! This is wrong—it angers the God Stone. Women are weak. They only exist to serve men and to make warriors with their bellies. Women are unclean! Women are the weakness that makes men weak. The God Stone has created men to be strong, women to be weak. A woman cannot hunt, a woman cannot fight. A woman cannot speak against any man, be he her mate or her son or father. The God Stone despises that which is weak. The God Stone punishes that which is weak. Worship the God Stone or die, and be the dust of nothing. Women must stay with women, and be used only for serving men and making warriors with their bellies. The God Stone commands this."

The women all stared at the ground, their eyes worried but obedient. Girls old enough to understand the new Mogan blinked their eyes in fear, not knowing how to behave.

"This woman who kneels before you is disgrace!" Regga yelled. "She will suffer the punishment of any who defies the commands of the God Stone!"

The woman had been bound and gagged, lest she show some last courageous defiance. Her hair had been shorn and burned; her body broken from torture. She had been made as wretched and ugly as a creature could be made. She studied the ground with dull eyes that only wanted death, oblivious to the crowd of hating faces that awaited her last moment.

Regga, mindful of the drama, held it at bay and let the dense silence go on. Left of him stood Karas, the brother of Thais, who stared coldly at the distance. He did not approve of this public killing of the woman who had allegedly spoken words against the God Stone. What had this to do with wars against the enemy? They should be fighting, not wasting their time in some ritual killing of a woman.

Yet Regga was the new Mogan of the South Menkala; and for now he was the most powerful being on the plains. The two men who had stood in his way, Xarran, chieftain of the Southern Menkala, and Mogan Cariolus had both died of mysterious illnesses. That in itself was not extraordinary: the Menkala god of illness, Iliona, killed more than all other dangers that were a daily reality. Iliona often struck whole tribes, leaving a fearsome toll of corpses. This was the way of things. The death of Chieftain Xarran, of Mogan Cariolus, of this woman—all were due to the will of the God Stone. Regga's cleverness and ruthlessness ensured this.

Karas had kept his silence, but he could see a change in Regga, how the power of the new god had turned his eyes so quickly to blood rage, how the sudden adoration of so many had put a madness into him. So it had been with Cariolus, before Iliona had reminded him with a fever and slow death, that he was not a god.

Finally Regga raised his arms: "We give this sacrifice to Menka, who lives in the God Stone—who lives in the new temple! We give this sacrifice to any who refuses to worship the One Most Powerful God of the Temple!"

A young Menkala warrior stood at ready next to the kneeling, broken woman. At Regga's command he lifted a great stone ax and with a swift swing the young warrior severed the woman's head. A chant erupted, then a mad cheer. The women all keened when Regga lifted the head for all to see; but many wore fearful eyes.

"To any who do not believe!" Regga roared out. "To any who refuse to worship the God Stone!"

Karas kept a quiet face as the roar went out to the empty prairie, startling birds and beasts to silence. He only wanted to restore honor to his family; that was his vow to Menka. That could only be done by killing his brother, the great traitor. He was older than Thais, and many times in childhood their father had pitted them against one another for his personal amusement. Always Thais had found a way to out-smart and defeat him, and Karas would be whipped for his weakness.

There never was love in the families of the Menkala. Love is weakness. The only true strength is hatred, and that was what drove Karas, more than any god, more than any stone from the sky. Spies had informed him that Thais, now a great figure in the Tolai mountain tribe, had a mate and that she had given him a child. How perfect it would be to destroy them as Thais watched, to avenge all past humiliations, and then to see the blood of his brother drip slowly into the earth.

Let Regga have his power and glory; Karas' mind was on simple revenge.

Eleven . . .

Shaman Haldana summoned Thais into his cave space. The holy man had smoked the spear-head plant (Thais could plainly smell it in the air, a skunkish odor that mated with the smells of mountain incense and the tart mixtures used to paint the cave walls).

"Enter?"

"Yes, Thais, please enter."

Thais spread the holy man's deer skin door and sat down across Haldana's fire.

The shaman was not quite of this world. His eyes seemed mystified—what the Mogans of the Menkala called "Noal se colo" (between the worlds). Haldana stared into his small fire.

"You are troubled," Thais said.

Haldana looked up sharply at him. "Many dreams have been coming to my mind. So many visions, since the snake man came. And since Mira brought the white wolf."

"What visions?"

The shaman sighed, an old man trying to understand a new world. "I cannot know for certain. This man from the far desert tells of the rise of the new god—Menka."

"Menka is not a new god," Thais said. "Menka is the Menkala god of war. It is said in the old tales that this is how the Menkala got their name."

"Now they say this god has conquered the other gods and stands as the only god. I did not believe what the snake man said."

"He does not believe it."

"But now dreams come to me; of an all-powerful god who conquered all other gods and now reigns supreme. Could this be true?"

Thais studied the fire: "Our scouts tell us that—for the Menkala—it is true. Menka now rules the sky and land."

"Because a God Stone fell from the sky."

"Yes."

"How can such things be explained?"

"Some things cannot be explained, Shaman."

Haldana seemed lost. He had foretold the changing of the world. The Witch of Conai had foretold it. The holy men of the Four Tribes had foretold it. But now they seemed dazed that it was happening.

"A great god—a great magic from the sky," Haldana said. "The One who sweeps away the balance of life; one who conquers all life and all meaning, and everything! I see in my dreams and god-visions One God who is all-powerful. One God who will sweep life away with a twitch of the finger. A God who shakes me awake from my dreams not calm and joyful as before—but with fear that I have never felt."

"So said the witch, when I last spoke to her."

Haldana shot Thais a stare. "Why did Zianna want to talk to you about this?"

"You know, Shaman. The witch knows what I cannot speak."

"But I can: you do not believe the gods exist. This Menka is not real."

"My belief is not good to speak. I spoke aloud of it once and it nearly got me killed. My beliefs do not matter."

"Who can deny the power of the gods?"

"The gods are powerful because people believe they are powerful. That gives the gods all power, whether they are true or not. People believe gods exist—that is the true power. You know this; you practice this."

"Tell me of Menka," Shaman said. "Who came to your tribe in a blaze of fire."

"Menka is the strongest god of the Menkala. He is the god of war. After the Menkala have slaughtered a tribe they stake the heads of the enemy then burn the tribe to the ground. While they do this they pray to Menka. I was made to worship Menka—we all were."

"Pray for what?"

Thais shrugged. "To give more cruelty, to give more savagery; to give more death."

"Is this what the world will come to be?"

Thais looked long into the shaman's fire. His eyes were sad, but sure: "It seems that this is what the world will become—gods or no gods."

"What of the white wolf?"

Thais smiled. "It seems that Hosho Dona—the white wolf—will be giving Mira's Wolf puppies before long."

"Will they be magic things?"

"Yes, they will be magic things. The pups will be magic things."

"How do you know this?"

"I know Wolf, Mira's dog. I have seen what he can do when he is needed the most. These pups may do more for us than any gods."

Twelve . . .

The expedition to the desert, led by Thais and Malek-So-Conyo, the Ooma scout, set off south on the river trail. This was familiar land, and when the hunters stopped to rest Mira played with Shana on the pebbled river bank.

"Soon we will be in a strange land, my love," she said.

Shana smiled. "Love Mama!"

"I love you too, Little Papoose. We are off on an adventure. We are!"

Shana looked up. Her nose curled. "I'm afraid, Mama!"

Mira's heart ached. "I know you are. Mama's afraid too."

"Daddy's not afraid."

Mira stroked Shana's long brown hair. "It may be that Daddy is afraid, but he does not show it. It is all right to be afraid, Shana. But look out at the world, My Papoose. Look at it! I want you to see it—I want you to be afraid."

Thais strode up to them, smiling, and knelt to hug Shana. Wolf was trotting down the river, sniffing at ground squirrel holes.

"We will be at the Conai before sundown. A scout Golthis sent up tells me that a great feast awaits us."

"It will be good to see Jella. Now the Cold Days are over, I feel better in my heart."

"It was a gentle winter," Thais said. "Our Ooma friend says that it will be many days beyond the Salotai before we cross the short mountain passes into the desert."

"And past where the Palotai lived—where Adela lived." Mira shuddered. "I mourn those who are gone, who will never be seen again. These days it seems that death is everywhere."

"There is nothing but to go on." Thais kissed her cheek.

"I wish Turok had lived."

"We may have other children, My Love. We may have many children."

"I hope it is so."

The Conai welcomed them with a great feast. Children ran in play, Shana waddling after them. Shaman Haldana met with the shaman of the Conai, Sandana. Mira sat with Jella and helped make a huge salad of mountain greens sprinkled with ground pinion nuts and garnished with mushrooms and the hearty mountain mint. It eased Mira's heart watching her little girl splashing with the bigger children in the river shallows, Shana picking colored pebbles out of the burbling water.

"I feel weak mourning the baby I lost," Mira said at last. "I should leave the dead baby behind and go on."

"You will never leave your dead baby behind," Jella said. "I lost mine many seasons ago, and I have not left her behind."

"Do you know that she was a girl child?"

"No. Do you know that Turok was a boy?"

Mira smiled. "I wish you would come with us on this journey. It's hard to speak to men."

"Yes it is. But I'm not going on this journey. Let my mate have the adventure; that is all he talks about." Jella looked at her. "I can look after Shana."

"No. I want her to see the far desert."

Jella looked up at the Conai caves. "Your shaman and mine meet with the witch. They are speaking of the changing of the world, and how we must change."

"Yes," Mira said.

"Will you speak to the witch?"

"I hope to."

"She has been keeping to her cave." Jella looked away across the river. She shuddered. "I'm afraid, Mira! Of this new beast-god, and what we have done by going to the Short Hills. I am afraid, Mira."

"Yes, I am too."

"Will those monsters come again to our mountains? When will this terrible thing be over?"

"I don't know." Mira stared up at the cave of the witch, where the holy men and

Zianna were speaking of the God Stone. "I wish I could stay here, where Shana plays with your children—where I have you to talk to."

"I wish you would. But you can't." Jella smiled sadly at her. "You must go to the far lands of the earth. You must see the monsters—Mira, the Wolf-girl."

"I saw much death in those Cold Days. And then I saw Dona give birth to five puppies. They are only dogs, I know; but somehow they helped to heal my heart. When we return from the desert, when Dona's pups are weaned, you must let each of your children pick one to raise."

"Ha. You know what my mate thinks of wolves."

"Golthis will change his mind about dogs, when he sees how they protect your children with their very lives. Dona did not want me to take Shana away, and she made as much trouble as her big belly would let her."

Jella laughed. "My mate calls them scavengers, who eat more than they're worth and steal what they can."

"Yet I saw your giant mate—when he thought no one was looking—rub Wolf on the back and feed him pemmican."

"He spoke to me of how Wolf went into battle with them, and how Wolf put fear and amaze into the Menkala. My mate respects anything that fights. But a wolf cub for each of my children?"

"They will grow as Wolf did; they will protect your children and your tribe."

"There was a day when we did not need protection. Golthis is inflamed with adventure and warfare. He has come to love it."

"So, I fear, has my mate."

"I long for the days when we were safe."

"Jella, I do not believe we were ever safe; we only thought we were."

"What happened to the far south Palotai—what happened to your friend . . ."

"The world as it is," Mira said.

The Witch of Conai welcomed Mira into her cave. Zianna looked weary; but she smiled, and her eyes, as always, were bright and fierce.

"The Hosho Dona has given birth," she said.

Mira sat down and let her eyes adjust to the gloom. "Yes. Five pups; none all white, but some with white spots."

"That is enough." The witch studied her with strangely gentle eyes. "You have seen death in those Cold Days, Mira."

"Yes. My mother died and the child in me died."

"And you cared for them—you cared very much, did you not?"

Mira returned her strange eyes. "Yes, I did."

"Do you care for me?"

Mira was startled by the question. Zianna seemed a wooden totem, almost hidden in the dark. Her face a graven image.

"Yes," Mira said.

"It is good to know that at the end of one's days. When I go to meet the gods, many will be relieved, I suspect; few if any will mourn me."

"I will."

"The gods call to me at last," said the witch, looking away. "What song, I wonder, will be of me and the dark days I lived." She tried to laugh, but her voice was hoarse, and she seemed to have trouble finding breath. She coughed instead, and when she had gasped herself still, she took a ragged breath and said, "When you return—if you return—I will be with the gods."

"I hope it is not so," Mira said. "There is so much I want to learn from you."

"You have learned all that you can learn from me. You will never be a witch, Mira. You must have hatred in your heart to be a witch; old hard undying hate. You must live to put fear into people. I could teach you how to make spells that will frighten people to true death. I could teach you how to make poisons and how to give them to the unexpecting. I can teach you how to never attend feasts and celebrations so that joy would not be spoiled. I can teach you how to be powerful and feared. But you, Mira, have learned all that I can truly teach you."

A day later the expedition of Conai and Tolai traveled south down the river, stopping at the Emotai village to acquire more hunters; then on south to the Salotai. The expedition grew to an impressive force, and Mira was proud marching with them into the unknown.

When at last they passed by the old home of the Palotai, Mira gave a gift of flowers to her girlhood friend, murdered by the Menkala, at the time when her life and her womanhood were just beginning.

"I wish you were alive, Adela." Mira knelt to put the flowers on the river bank, where she was sure Adela had knelt to pick up stones and shells. "I wish you were here, and we could laugh and show off our children and talk about our lives. I miss you, Adela—by all the gods, I miss you!"

"Why Mama cry?" Shana was at her shoulder, upset. Wolf, hovering nearby, whined at the smell, as if the memory were touching his instincts.

"I lost a friend here, that's all. I'll quit crying."

"Mama, where are we going?"

"See there, to the south? That is where we are going. Your Masha has never been there, and even your Dasha has not seen those lands."

"I'm scared, Mama!"

Mira smiled at the south. "So am I, Papoose. Goodbye, Adela. When I speak to you, may you hear my words. The world calls us south."

Thirteen . . .

Thais walked with the Ooma scout, Malek-So-Conyo, down the river from the main party of hunters. The air was dry here, flowing up from the south desert. The dense pine smell gave way to the milder odors of scrub brush and sage. Beyond, the fertile mountains turned bare, the horizon ruled by stone and sand. They were entering the land of the Ooma.

"You eat snakes," Thais said abruptly. He saw the man's eyes shift. "Do they taste good?"

Malek-So-Conyo gave him a cautious look.

"I know you understand river speak." Thais smiled. "I knew it when I first met you, when we ate together that long ago."

"You good people," the scout said, after a pause. "But one must gather knowing. One must keep secrets in this new world."

"True. And I will tell no one. Ke osso se Menkala?"

"Le."

Thais nodded. "You have wandered farther and wider than I have. I do not know your tongue."

"Many tongues in the desert. I know not all of them, but maybe one day I will teach you mine. We Ooma of the far north desert. Below us desert goes on past any eyes, to tribes that only know the bison in old stories and songs."

"It is good that our tribes are united and at peace. It is not good that such distance separates us."

Malek-So-Conyo looked at him. "You wish to make war with Menkala—this is true? This is why you want explore."

"Yes. Not war this season, but maybe the next. There must be war, and we must be prepared."

"Against your people, the Menkala."

"They are not my people. And I do not want war with them. But if they are not destroyed, our tribes will be. You have seen what god gifts the bison bring; how they make the Ooma so much stronger."

"Yes. Some in my tribe want fight for bison. But Menkala are too strong."

"Now they are. It is very bad that the north and south Menkala are united. But they worship death, and that means they will always weaken themselves and seek to destroy themselves, if they can find no other. They are powerful now, on the plains; but they will grow weaker, and we can grow stronger."

"That is why this trip to my land."

"Yes. To see your secret passes and to meet your people."

Malek gave Thais a worried blink. "We are not warlike. Brave, but we do not like killing other men."

"So it is with the mountain tribes. But there is nothing for it; we cannot keep the hunters from the bison. They have beheld the Great Herd and they will risk all to harvest it. The people of my birth know this. They will destroy any tribe that risks hunting the bison."

"So it has always been with the Ooma. It is different now. The Menkala have the new god. They have the power of the God Stone."

"It seems to be their strength; but it may become their weakness. If we prepare and understand one another, the Ooma and mountain tribes could win. Not this season, or even the next. It is more important to you than us."

"How you mean?"

"The Menkala have invaded the mountains two times and were slaughtered. They fear the mountains and the gods within. But what is to stop them from moving south into your desert?"

"They have never ventured into our lands. Not much food, you will see. Why they come to the desert?"

"To destroy you." Thais looked to the south. "We travel to meet your people because the old ways cannot go on. Do your holy men speak of the changing of the world?"

"They do."

"Then we all must change. And it would be better if we change together."

"We do not steal from others," Malek-So-Conyo said. "It is against our gods to steal."

"We are the same. The mountain tribes do not want the desert."

"We do not want the mountains."

"But that is not the way of the Menkala. I was born and raised Menkala. They will battle the eastern Paw-Nee, and when they push them away they will move south against your Ooma. We will all have to fight the Menkala, together or not. We have a chance if we fight them together."

"My people have a great fear of the God Stone. They fear that He will destroy our gods, those we have worshipped beyond memory."

"It is not a matter of gods," Thais said. "It is only a matter of bison."

Fourteen . . .

Nekena, the famous Northern Menkala scout, was tall and muscular and very crafty. Thais knew of him; a man able to run forever across any terrain; a man who never seemed to tire. He was sent on the most extreme and dangerous missions, to gain information on enemy movements.

He could live indefinitely on mice and pinion nuts. He could leap over boulders and vanish like smoke in the wind; he could find water in the driest places. He was a legend throughout the plains. He had quickly embraced the cult of the God Stone, was an immediate fanatic, and now spied for Regga, the Great Mogan.

This night he appeared out of the darkness, giving his exhausted code word to the startled Menkala sentries, and entered the Menkala camp, where the tall spire of rock stabbed the sky. He gorged himself on bison meat, drank more than three gourds of water and rested his shivering legs. Regga and Karas were summoned and Nekena gave his report:

"An Ooma scout is leading them south. It seems they want to meet with the Ooma at the edge of the desert."

"Did you see my brother Thais?'"

Nekena traded looks with Karas. "Yes. He does much scouting for the mountain force."

"How many?" Regga asked.

"More than 100. They bring men from all the mountain tribes. They bring their chieftains and their Mogans."

"A good time to attack them," Karas said. "Wipe out the whole of them."

"We could not get enough warriors there in time," Regga said.

"On their return journey, when they are worn by travel."

"Maybe." Regga looked at the scout. Though a Northern Menkala, Nekena could be trusted. "Do you know, Nekena, why they travel south?"

"I suspect that they are making plans with the Ooma for war. I never got close enough to hear them; but they spoke to the Ooma with hands, and I could read them. They know of the God Stone; they know that we are united under the One God. They know there will be war, and they are preparing for it."

"Good," Karas said. "Is my brother's mate with him?"

"Yes, and their child. A girl named Shana."

"We have heard of a Hosho Dona," Regga said.

"They speak of it. And a wolf does move with them; but it is not white."

"My brother and his child are on this expedition," Karas said.

"No matter that." Regga gave him a look. "We invaded the mountains to kill those people—and they killed us. We have seen what the mountains do to our warriors; how the mountains take the legs and lungs and rob us of the strength to fight. I will not make the mistakes of Mogan Cariolus."

"We can attack them at the north desert," Karas said. "They will be weak from their journey."

"They will be with the Ooma, our enemies and now their friends. What do you think, Nekena?"

"It is a long trek, with no sure victory. I do not know the passes that far to the south, and I believe their Ooma scout does. I have heard of that man." Nekena looked at Karas. "I could have killed your brother."

"No. That is for me."

"You never truly knew your brother," Regga said. "But I did. Thais will not be taken by surprise. He will make an army that will challenge us. He knows of what we speak right now. It could be that he lures us to the desert."

"We have the God Stone," Karas said.

"And I will speak to the God Stone. Thais will make a danger to us, but in the future. More danger comes to us from the east and the north—and it comes to us now."

"We angered Menka long ago, when we let my brother escape judgment," Karas muttered.

<u>Regga gave him a look, and Karas was reminded of the death of Chieftain Xarran and Mogan Cariolus.</u>

He turned to the scout. "When you have rested and strengthened, Nekana, return to this mountain force, and find what you can about it

Fifteen . . .

Malek-So-Conyo led the expedition south, and Mira was surprised at how curvy the river became. They were marching downward, she sensed, below the great peaks she had always known into very rocky and sandy mountains; piles of boulders, many of them. Shana attached to her hand, Mira studied the new terrain. She had never seen a land so lush as the Short Hills—she had never seen one so craggy and barren as this.

At a massive peak that burst into the sky, and changed the course of the very river, the Ooma scout ordered that the expedition must slow down and face the dry air and the sun of these hills.

They wandered into a dry, prickled world. Tiresome mountains of bare rock defined the distance. Powder rose up from the moccasins of the marching hunters. On the third day of dust and sun and boulders, the hunters killed a great bear, and Mira stole some of its fat to smear on herself and Shana. So dry was the air that Mira itched even below the bear fat.

Great dead flatlands lay between the mountains. Cacti and tough shrubs shivered in the dusty wind. Shana stumbled over the powdered ground, Mira yanking her away from the many cacti that spread their needles to the glaring sun. They wore deer skin dresses and deer skin moccasins that came up to the knee. Mira had never seen such ugly land. Grasses stood in clumps, ground squirrels peeped out of the tawn dirt. Thais warned her of deadly snakes and lizards and scorpions. She kept a close eye on Shana, as did the Ooma scout—as did Wolf, who sniffed at the dry wind and stared away into this new world.

At a pool in the river Mira caught fish and fried them over a fire of thistle. How strange that here the very bushes broke free of the earth and waddled strangely in the wind, looking like living things in the bright moonlight, as if they were strolling merrily northward.

She washed herself and Shana in the river. It was late, and the full moon sat in the west in a faint smear of clouds. She should be weary from all the marching and work; but she was bewitched by this clear dry land. She put Shana to sleep and spread out on her bison robe. She stared up at the stars, so bright and sparkly that she felt the gods.

Thais appeared, sweaty and rough-smelling from scouting. He lay next to her and stared with her at the stars. "I never sleep much; but you should sleep, Mira. This is a long and strange trail."

"I can't sleep," she said. "This new land—and what strange lands in the world! Can they go on forever?"

"I do not know, My Love; they seem to. Malek says that in only three days we will meet with his people. They traveled north to meet with us, a good sign—I hope. So we will only see a sliver of this desert land."

"I feel monsters all around me in this land. But I have seen none."

"The monsters of the Short Hills are very big; the monsters of the desert are very small. You, Shana, we are all in danger of these things; so you must be careful where you step. Snakes that rattle, scorpions that sting; spiders and lizards that are poison. All of these little things will kill you, if you're not very careful."

"Or Shana."

Mira shuddered. She looked down the winding river to the south, where more stone mountains, brown and purple, rose from the dust. "How can things live here?"

Thais hugged her and kissed her neck. "They would ask us the same about the mountains."

The expedition climbed eastward into a winding canyon. Malek climbed a mountain with Thais, and they studied the skies before loping down and ordering the men forward. Thais and the Ooma scout met with Mira and Shana and Wolf as they entered a serpentine corridor, a narrow path twisting around dry mountains.

"Why did you climb up there?" Mira asked. "To look for Menkala?"

"No," Thais said. "To look for clouds."

"Clouds?" Mira looked at Malek. He was knelt down, giving Shana a blue-green pebble from the top of the mountain.

Malek signed to her, of storms and a death-rush of water in the canyons.

"I know you speak my language," Mira said.

Malek gave Thais a shocked look.

"He did not tell me," Mira said. "I heard you whispering to Shana in river tongue."

"Shana reminds me of my daughter. She is Lian, and she is about Shana's age." Malek smiled at her. "I hope my wife, who is called Keal, brings Lian to this meeting. Then I will settle down with my mate and my children. I have traveled too long and too far."

"There will be war," Thais reminded him. "There will be a need for a scout as good as you."

Malek looked sadly down at Shana. "I pray, Little One, that I will see you and my Lian holding hands, being best friends, kneeling together at the river to pick up colored stones. For all my travels, that is only a little to ask."

Thais shook his head at him. "You know this language better than you ever let on."

"And so—I suspect—did you."

"When we meet your tribe, I hope to make friends with your mate Keal," Mira said. "What are the women in your tribe like?"

"They are harder than the mountain women. The sun dries out their faces. But I think that makes them the more beautiful."

Sixteen . . .

Mira marched, holding Shana's hand, with her father and Shaman Haldana. This sinuous canyon scared her as it gradually narrowed and they made their way downward. The walls of rock grew taller, as if squeezing the expedition between their granite shoulders.

Etain and Haldana both walked with their eyes to the uneven ground, often stumbling over the rocks that were everywhere. The two men were very weary, their old faces blasted by this hot desert wind. Malek had said that beyond this canyon would be a high table of land; and beyond that the valley where the Ooma tribe waited. Thais, Golthis, Malek and a young Salotai hunter named Andar had gone forth to meet them; but was this a trap? Would Thais return?

Mira was worried; all of the mountain hunters were worried, their eyes glancing up at the stone walls that seemed to move closer with each curve of the canyon. Water had made this place, the tales said. But where was water in this land? She carried Shana down the rock-round path, praying the next turn of this frightening place would give them wide plains. She felt entombed. She put her mind into a trance and simply walked on, staring at the dangerous ground.

"A very weary land," Etain finally panted.

"A weary land," Shaman Haldana agreed. The holy man would stare up at the canyon walls and study paintings that seemed impossible: some distant race had painted pictures far up on the flat walls. Snakes, men, antelope, lizards decorated the canyon in forgotten paints of red, yellow, black. Haldana's eyes asked how it could have been done.

The petroglyphs followed them down to a corridor of light. At last came the end of the canyon, and Mira hugged her daughter.

"Look at that, Shana! Look where we've come!"

Mira was relieved when Thais loped into the canyon, with Wolf alongside, tired but excited. The hunters all cheered him and slapped his back. But they were worried. Beyond this pass they would meet the Snake People, and the Snake People were many.

He came up to Mira and Shana, hugged and kissed them. His face was sandy and salty. "My girls!" he said. "How are you holding up?"

"We're fine. Tired, dirty and scared—but fine. You look worn, My Mate. And Wolf looks very dusty."

Thais grinned. "It was a good meeting with the Ooma. A stream runs down below these canyons, and then wide desert. We will meet our new friends where a pile of great boulders rises. Many paintings on the rocks. It is a holy place."

"Are they many?" Mira asked.

"Yes. More than a thousand, I guess."

Mira was shocked. "What if they led us here to destroy us?"

"Believe me, Love, I have thought of that from the day we left. But no. They are good people. They have prepared a great celebration, a great feast for us. They know that without friendship and trust, we will all die."

Wolf lay tired as Shana scrubbed his face.

"Good Wolf," she said.

"He met dogs from the Ooma," Thais said. "They are all coyote dogs, half the size of Wolf; so he felt powerful among them. Malek's mate brought their little one, Lian; so Shana will have a friend to make."

"Did Wolf behave?"

"Yes. The Ooma were disappointed that he was not the white one."

Thais took Shana into his arms and they walked out of the canyon and into glaring sun and a brown-grey mesa of boulders and cacti and what her mother had called witch hair. Swirls of dust spun in the dry distance. Mira beheld a distance of magnificent beauty. She could see below the mesa, spread out over the valley, the tee pees of the Ooma people—cones of willow and antelope hide dotting the valley. And the sparkling stream where Ooma women washed and bathed.

"Look where we have come!" she marveled. "Look, Shana! Look, Wolf; look where we have come."

"Many in the Ooma have heard of you," Thais said. "The Wolf Girl of the far mountains, who hunted the bison and fought the Menkala. You will be marveled at."

"I barely speak their tongue," Mira said. "I'm not very good with the hand speak."

"That will only make you more mysterious." He smiled. "They speak of Hosho Dona, and Malek assured them that the pure white wolf is true."

Mira stared at the distance. Strange plumes of smoke puffed from a stone peak. Not dust, but clouds of smoke.

"That is how the Ooma signal," Thais said. "Their scouts signal with smoke."

"How can they do that?"

"I do not know. Somehow they know how to speak with smoke; and how to read."

Golthis strode down from the Conai hunters and approached them. "Well, Thais, here we are. I didn't expect to see so many snake warriors. They are very many, and we are very few."

"If they want to destroy us, they can," Thais said.

Malek came loping up the mesa, smiling. Mira admired his stamina, his bare courage against the earth.

"My friends," he said, catching his breath. "My people welcome the mountain tribes, who defeated the Menkala. We welcome Golthis, the Great Giant. We welcome Mira, the Wolf-Girl with so much courage. We welcome you all."

Mira made a weary smile. "I think we will all need to rest."

"Of couse. Respected places of rest await you. And a giant bison bed for you, Giant of the South."

Golthis feigned surprise. "You speak my tongue?

"Forgive me, my friend." Malek smiled. He turned to Mira: "My mate Keal is excited to meet you. And my daughter Lian is excited to play with Shana along the stream."

"I hope to see Keal," Mira said. "And to meet your people."

"What do the smoke signals say?" Thais asked.

"Menkala scouts." Malek shrugged. "They are few; I expected them."

"Yes. I did too."

"Our warriors will drive them away. We are safe here."

The mountain tribes marched down to meet the desert tribes. Golthis, a colossal man against the slender, whip-like men of the Ooma, earned a great cry of reknown, and many scampered up to touch him. He played along by looking fierce and scaring the children.

The Ooma were raw-dressed, Mira saw. A starved people with eyes of hard hope. She held Thais' hand as she walked among the welcoming crowd. She smiled at this new tribe, this new race of people.

She saw in their eyes a wonder as they watched her pass. Many of the women reached out to touch her. Suddenly a beautiful young woman appeared before her in an antelope dress, a necklace of strange shells about her neck.

Malek hugged this woman. A child peeped out from behind them and smiled shyly at Shana.

"This is your mate, Keal?" Mira asked.

"Yes. We ask that your family stay with us," Malek said. "A ceremonial tee pee has been set up for you. My tee pee is close. Keal asks if you will accept our homes."

"With thanks," Mira said. "We will be honored to stay with you."

Malek grinned. He translated to Keal, who smiled at Mira and motioned her forward. Thais put Shana down, Lian took her hand, and they were instant friends.

Mira was led to a large tee pee. She crawled gratefully into soft deer blankets. She was exhausted. Keal touched her hand and smiled at her.

Sleep, she signed.

Mira lay with Shana and fell into a long dreamless sleep. She came awake late in the night and stared into the darkness. Shana made child snores against her. Then she could hear the quiet movements of the Ooma camp. She jumped up from the deer blanket, and Thais' rough hand touched her back.

"Shhh, My Love," he whispered. "Go back to sleep. Rest up for the feast."

"The feast."

"It will begin tomorrow. We will celebrate with our new friends."

"The Ooma. I have not even washed, Thais; I was too tired. I'm gritty and smelly."

"We all are. That is nothing here."

"Where is my father, and Shaman Haldana?"

"They sleep in a tee pee nearby. It seems we are very respected guests."

His soft voice comforted her, and Mira smiled into the darkness. "I like the tee pees. Maybe one day we will live in one."

"They are good for a tribe that travels. I grew up in a tee pee. We learned to take them down and set them up very quick."

"At sunrise I will have to wash my clothes, and me. I will have to wash Shana."

"Keal will take you to a place."

"I hope they like me."

Thais kissed her in the dark. "They will love you. Now sleep, My Love."

Mira fell back into the soft darkness and into a strange sleep.

During the feast and celebration Golthis could be heard bellowing out laughter. Mira saw him pounding Malek fondly on the back as the Ooma gathered round, proud to be near the Giant of the South. Shaman Haldana and Chieftain Etain sat with the chieftains and holy men of the Ooma tribes; Shana and Lian were playing with twin coyote puppies, cradling them and showing them off as babies.

Mira sat with Keal and the Ooma women. She was quickly learning how to speak with her hands, a common skill in the desert tribes. She was amazed at the artistic talents of these people. Their bowls of clay were coated with a beautiful enamel, decorated with swirls and stripes of eggshell and ochre. The jewelry of these women! Gorgeous shells; beads of alabaster bone. The shells shone rainbow in the sun, like some of the birds of the mountains, when sunlight would catch them.

Keal signed: *The shells are from the great water of salt. Water that goes beyond the eyes.*

Mira had seen mountain lakes, but she could not imagine water beyond her eyes. Thais came loping down from the mesa, accompanied by an Ooma scout. The desert tribe relied on Thais, she knew—because he was once a Menkala. Thais sat down next to her, smiling at the admiring women, who immediately gave him a bowl of milky liquid. He accepted it gratefully, but only sipped.

"What is that?" Mira asked. "I see Golthis drinking much of it."

"That is why he is so happy." Thais smiled at the Giant, who was bellowing out laughter with his new warrior friends. "It is a juice from the cactus; it makes one happy."

"Let me taste it."

"But not too much. It makes you stumbly and fogs your mind."

"My mind is already fogged." Mira took the bowl of cloudy liquid from her mate and drank. It was a sweet-tasting beverage that had a strange burn to it. Mira made a mild gasp and handed the bowl back. The Ooma women all began giggling.

"It is strong—and it bites your throat," Mira said.

"The more **you drink, the less it bites," Thais said. He drank down the cactus juice, and an Ooma woman was quick to refill it.**

"The cactus must be a plant of great magic," Mira said. "My mother told me of cactus buttons that take one into the world of gods."

"I'm sure Shaman Haldana will eat one tonight with the holy men of the Ooma."

Mira looked out over the dry plain, where the desert people began preparing the feast. Racks of deer and antelope were hung over cedar wood fires. Big reptiles and even snakes were carried on spears to be cooked. Desert hares, with the long legs and ears, birds of strange design came to the fires, and soon the familiar smell of bison meat drifted over the valley.

Keal touched Mira's arm. She presented her with a bowl of the cactus juice. Mira smiled and accepted it, seeing that the Ooma women were amused. Then Keal presented her with a gift, and Mira was stunned. It was a beautiful elk robe with a white wolf painted in the center. Keal spread her arms out to say that all of the Ooma women had made it to honor her. Mira's eyes grew tears as she touched her heart and bowed.

"They made this for me?" she asked Thais.

"And a smaller robe for Shana. Hers is decorated with the green pebbles that are sacred to the Ooma."

Mira stroked the elk robe. "What can I say? I have brought no gifts."

"You have brought yourself; and you have brought our daughter."

Mira drank the cactus juice as the Ooma women giggled and chattered among themselves. Mira handed the ornate bowl to Keal and stroked her white wolf robe. She began to feel strange, as she had in her rite of womanhood, when in Shaman Haldana's cave she had smoked the spear-head plant. Happiness drifted into her. She watched Shana and Lian giggling and playing hand signs. She wished the world could stop right here and now, in peace and celebration. May the world stop here, she prayed, knowing that it would not.

Bison meat scented the desert air. Golthis bellowed out a laugh and took another bowl of the cactus juice. Thais smiled at the celebration, as the Ooma men and women prepared to dance. Then he studied the highlands, purple in the dying sun, where Ooma and mountain scouts watched the distance.

Mira felt pleasantly numb. As the desert sun fell into the far mountains, turning the sky into smears of pink, yellow, purple, she relaxed and smiled. Mira had been as nervous as a squirrel on this journey—she didn't know why. Now, in the far south desert of the songs she felt herself relax and rejoice.

Keal gestured with the bowl, and Mira smiled and nodded. Shana and Lian came running up from the stream, the coyote pups following. Wolf sniffed at them; then stood like a guardian statue, his solemn eyes staring into the gathering night.

"I must explore this place!" Mira looked out with drunken eyes at the celebration, the songs of joy and adventure that rose into the dry desert night. "I must find what magic things grow here!"

"Eat, Mira," Thais said. "It is not good to drink of the cactus on an empty stomach."

"Drink with me, My Love! Never have we been to such a land. And we may never see it again!" She hugged a joyful Keal: "Shana, is this not exciting?"

"Yes, Mama."

"I cannot drink too much tonight," Thais said. "I need to have a sure mind."

"Why?" Mira frowned at him. "We are being watched. The Menkala are watching us?"

"Yes, Mira; they are."

"Damn them! I would like to kill all of them!"

"All of them?" Thais smiled.

"Will they never leave us in peace? Will they never share the bison with us and let us have peace and celebration? Do they always have to spoil the world with their hate?"

"Yes, they do."

"I will fight them and kill them!"

"Yes, Mira, I believe you will."

The celebration went on into the night; but Mira saw it with dazed eyes. They put Lian and Shana to bed, and Mira and Keal went back into the fire-lit wonder. Keal danced with the Ooma women, who performed elaborate moves round one of the great bonfires. The desert valley rippled in firelight. Drunken laughter roared out, and dancers performed to the elemental drum logs and song.

Mira stared out at the spectacle. She held Thais' hand and thanked the gods of the desert. Her life had taken her where she always wanted to go, into the violent heart of the world.

"I wonder if Mother is watching us," she said to Thais. "It is said that the souls of those who pass watch over us." Mira stared into the spectacular glittering sky. "I wonder if my brother Elat sees us; if Adela is looking after Turok for us."

"Maybe we will find out one day, Mira. But this is not the day."

Her old friend Adela, dead more than two seasons, had only wanted a good mate and a life of peace in a safe place where she could raise children and grow old in quiet happiness. But that was not the world of this age. Monsters were out there beyond the light of fires; human monsters that seemed forever to carve the world with hate, and shape it with their death-gods.

Keal touched her on the arm and smiled at her. Keal made a fist and tapped her heart with it. Mira saw far figures up on the mesa, shadows under the full bright moon. They were Ooma sentries, and scouts of the Four Tribes. She understood that this was more than a celebration and feast. This was a preparation for war.

"What does this mean?" she asked Thais. "When Keal touches her heart with her fist?"

"It means courage."

Mira smiled at Keal and touched her fist to her heart.

Seventeen . . .

The Menkala scout had slipped and fallen down the mesa, breaking his leg. Ooma and Mountain warriors were charging quickly up the mesa, and the spies could not take the time to climb down and finish him.

"He will kill himself," Nekena said. "We must leave him."

But the wounded scout passed out before he could cut his own throat; the desert hunters found him, gathered him up and took him into the valley, where he caused a great stir.

Thais was summoned. He studied the man, surprised that he was alive.

"He is Menkala?" asked Malek.

"Yes. You got him before he could kill himself. What of the others?"

Andar, the mountain scout of the Salotai said, "He was below the mesa on a crag of rock. The rest escaped us. There were three of them."

"They must know that we unite for war," Malek said. "You must speak to this Menkala when he wakes."

"I'll try," Thais said. "But he will probably tell us nothing."

When the Menkala scout came to, he found himself surrounded. He stared up at Golthis and nodded respectfully. He looked at Chieftain Etain; then he looked at Thais, his eyes fierce with hate. Thais tried to speak to him, but the spy only spat on the ground.

"What should be done with him?" Etain asked.

"You should kill him," Thais said.

"What?"

Thais turned to Malek. "He will pretend to be weak and helpless; then fast as a cougar he will kill as many of you as he can before he dies."

"We took his weapons."

"No matter. His weapons are his hands."

"Can we get no information from this man?" Etain asked.

"No. If he speaks he will speak lies. He only waits to attack and kill." Thais looked at Malek. "Forgive me, my friend; but I am saving at least one of your lives."

Shocking everyone, Thais fell on the Menkala scout and savagely slashed his throat. All stood in silence and watched the scout die. Eyes shifted to Thais as the scout's life bubbled red into the sand.

"I have saved lives," he said. Wiping his knife free of blood, he turned and walked away.

"They are speaking of you," Mira said. "They say you killed that scout."

"Yes, I did, Mira. So that he would not kill our friends."

"His leg was broken. They say he was helpless."

"His leg was broken; but he was not helpless. No good could have come from keeping him alive. They must get used to killing Menkala."

Mira frowned. "What of the others?"

"The Ooma have sent men out to try and find them."

They stayed in the valley of the Ooma for many days. Mira watched Shana and Lian playing at the stream with other children. How simple life was for them, in a world of wonder and pretend. Mira's father had approved the plans of the Ooma and mountain warriors; they would play a waiting game, use their time together to plan and coordinate, train warriors to use new weapons, to use signals and strategies for future battles.

Thais stood with Etain, Golthis and Malek in the desert valley. Mountain warriors were training Ooma warriors to use the atlatl; the Ooma taught the use of the sling.

"It is impressive how they throw the rocks," Golthis admitted. "I still prefer my ax."

"You could not get close enough to use your ax," Malek said. "You would be brained and down."

"The sling is easy to make," Thais said. "And easy to carry. Only a sling and a pouch of stones. It is a hard weapon to master; but I think we should all learn what we can about how to use it."

"It would be handy." Etain watched the Ooma hunters, their arms whipping stones violently into cactus targets as the mountain hunters watched. "Kill a hare and make a sling of its hide. Then all you need do is gather stones from the ground."

"All of our warriors should train with the sling," Thais said. "As the Ooma should train with the atlatl. We have time on our side; every new weapon will help us. The Menkala look at the sling as a women's weapon, unworthy of a warrior. That might be an advantage."

"I see it," Golthis said. "These skinny warriors can smash brains with their rocks."

Scouts came in from the Short Hills with reports of raging warfare north of the distant Flat River. Inflamed by the God Stone, fanatic believers attacked weaker tribes, burning tee pees, taking slaves and murdering all who refused to kneel to the One God.

As the mountain tribes prepared for their homeward journey, Thais climbed the great mesa with Malek. The men studied a strange hazy east.

"This might be lucky for us," Malek said. "I do not think our party will be attacked."

"No."

Both men knew what the distant haze meant: a great wildfire was burning on the plains. The wind was pushing it northward.

"Maybe it will burn our enemies up." Malek grinned. "The winter was dry, so this is no surprise."

"The most feared thing on the plains," Thais said. "Fire that can out-run even the deer. Flames that turn the world black as far as the eyes. See the orange glow just above the earth? That is a vast one."

"The gods favor our alliance. The fire drives our enemies away from us."

"They are probably far east of the fire. Still, it may be good luck."

Mira hugged Keal and said goodbye. They were both teary-eyed. Shana and Lian bawled in one another's arms. Wolf said goodbye to his coyote friends and the mountain expedition entered the canyon pass, the corridor of petroglyphs that led back north into the high mountains.

Both sides of the alliance had agreed to establish a post in the foothills halfway between the Salotai and Ooma, and to set up communication lines of scouts. To also continue training in preparation for a possible war, in the spring after the Cold Days, with the Menkala nation.

They marched higher. In the distance rose Mira's beloved mountains, and on the second day they reached the river, the beautiful flowing god Mira had known since her birth.

"Did you like the Ooma, Shana?" she asked as they marched up the trail.

"Yes, Mama."

"Did you like Keal and Lian? Did you like the coyote pups?"

"I named mine Turok," Shana said, her innocent face smiling up.

"You did." Mira held back tears. "Well, my papoose; when we get back home there will be wolf puppies to play with! Dona's puppies. And think of the new land you've seen, and the good people we met."

"My best friend is Lian," Shana said.

"And my new friend is Keal; though we live far apart."

"We ate snake, Mama."

Mira laughed. "Yes, we did. And some lizard."

"I will tell Keane I ate snake," Shana said. "Lian showed me a snake in the water, and it scared me."

"And she showed you how to spot the green stones that are so pretty." Mira gazed back to the south where the desert lay, as if it were a dusty dream. "Now we climb back to our own homes, Shana; in the high mountains."

Thais went ahead of the troop, accompanied by Malek, Andar and other tough scouts. As they loped upward from tall places they could see the grey haze over the far Short Hills. The fire was enveloping the plains, killing thousands of animals and people. When evening fell, Mira climbed a boulder and saw the pink and grey east shimmering in distant smoke.

Thais had told her about such fires that sometimes raced across the Short Hills and the eastern plains, fires beyond any fire that ever raged along the river.

They marched north, and before she expected it Mira heard cheers from the valley below the southern mountains. They had reached the home of the Salotai; and here Malek said goodbye.

"Wolf-girl," he said to Mira. "You have honored my people. May you always be friends with my Keal."

"I will always be friends with Keal," she said.

"Shana—the cutest wolfling—may you be forever the friend of my daughter. Golthis, the Giant: you took many gourds of the cactus. Enjoy them. And if you join my people in battle, they will take courage from you and fight to be in the songs."

"If a fight has to come," Golthis said. "Then I will be in it."

Malek turned to Thais: "My friend; may we win this terrible thing that is coming."

"It will be like that fire out there."

"The terrible thing that all know is coming. Our chieftains, our warriors, our holy men all speak of what is to come."

"The attacks may come to you next." Thais frowned eastward. "We stand with you; and we have time. We must use this time; the fire pushes the South Menkala across the river, and together with the North they destroy what tribes they find up there, the Crow and Chen. When the fire is spent, they may cast their eyes south, toward you."

"We will be ready." Punching his fist to his heart, Malek bid farewell and went back south down the dry, prickly trail.

The mountain expedition marched into the Salotai village. Shaman Haldana met with the holy man of the Salotai, and Etain met with his old friend Tanas, Chieftain of the Salotai. Mira said hello to cousins and women she had grown up with, now Salotai women. She was weary, and grateful when Thais made a bed for them away from people. She snuggled against him, feeling his hardness.

"No, Shana. You should be sleeping by yourself."

"No, Daddy—I'm scared!"

"You cannot sleep with us, Shana," Mira said. "You stop being scared."

"I can't, Mama!" Shana began bawling. "I'm scared!"

Shana, finally worn out, slept against them. Then Wolf stomped in, wanting to sleep with them. Mira looked up at the familiar mountain sky. She listened to the river. "How still the sky," she said.

"I was hoping to try and make another baby," Thais said, pushing Wolf aside.

"I was too," Mira said. Under the mountain stars they fell asleep.

Eighteen . . .

When they approached the home of the Conai word came to them that the witch Zianna had died. It was seen as a good sign.

Mira was the only one to cry when they heard the news. Zianna finally at peace, Zianna telling her with those ancient eyes that they would never see each other again. A witch at the end of a hard life to have a soft death.

Mira mourned her because she had passed; but more, she regretted the secrets Zianna had taken with her.

"The last thing she said was that she had taught me all that she could teach me."

"Maybe that's true," Thais said.

"But she taught me nothing. I wanted to know her secrets. She went away with so many secrets."

"You shed tears for her, Mira, when others do not. That may be all that she asked of you. You loved her, in your way, and you miss her. Maybe that was her secret."

Nineteen . . .

"We are growing rich!" Regga spoke to the Menkala, Northern and Southern, gathered at the Sacred Temple. "We are united and again powerful. Again the Menkala rule the Short Hills. But Menka commands that we destroy all unbelievers."

Balam, Chieftain of the Northern Menkala, spoke up: "We chase them away from our bison—they run from us back to their lands, to grub for lizards and hares; to starve!"

A great cry rose up. Regga, mad from eating god medicines, felt the power ripple across the plains.

"They believe that they are safe in their own lands. But soon we will have the power to take their lands from them, as they tried to take ours from us. If they oppose us, they will be destroyed. If they bow to the One God, the God Stone, they will keep their lives as slaves to the Menkala."

A roar washed over Regga; the voices of a strange new power that had come to Earth in a spear of flame. His eyes grew fierce as he stared out at the Believers.

"Many enemies surround us!" he called out. "But we are forming the army of the True God. We have destroyed tribes north of the Flat River; the Chen and the Crow People. Their tee pees glow red and turn to ash. The skulls of unbelievers stare sightless at the sky. Their treasures we take; their people we make slaves. None can stand against us. The God Stone has given us power over all tribes."

Nekena had returned to report that the mountain tribes of Thais had met and feasted with the Ooma.

"We lost a scout," Nekena said. "And we barely skirted the great fire."

"Yes." Regga stared southwestward. "The glow approaches, and no sign of rain."

"It might be best to move as many people as possible north of the river," Nekana said.

"I wonder what this means." Regga stared to the west, where before the distant shapes of the mountains the horizon glowed red. "How have we sinned?"

"The plains are very dry this year," the scout said. "That is a greater fire than I have seen. We should move across the river and prepare to move even farther north. If the fire reaches here the bison will Kan Dala and destroy everything in their panic."

"So be it," Regga said. "For now the fire keeps us from the desert enemy." He stared at the distant mountains that rose into the sky; and where, Karas always said, the great danger rose. "And the west enemy."

You are planning war, my old friend, he thought. You were born knowing war, Thais. You build a force in the west mountains, and you build a force in the south desert. You seek to connect two great armies. The north people scamper down to kill bison and then to escape with meat and furs and bones and treasure. Those we meet we kill. But you wait.

"You know of Thais," Regga said.

"Of course," Nekena answered. "I have seen him with the river tribes, and the Ooma."

"What do you make of him?"

Nekena shrugged. "He is very respected."

"He is an unbeliever. He was always an unbeliever. The God Stone despises him."

"I would have liked to fight him and kill him; but Chieftain Karas forbids it."

"Karas wants his brother's life for himself. Karas has many bones left in his throat."

"We saw them training with slings."

"Cowards." Regga scowled. "Did you see the Giant?"

"Yes. He got very drunk on cactus and tried to dance with the Ooma warriors. These tribes are now friends," he said pointedly.

"They dance, they sing, they laugh. All a mockery to the One God. These celebrations, these feasts—all signs that our enemies are weak."

"Yet they are uniting," Nekena said.

Regga's eyes were crazed. He stared madly into the west, where the smoke of the great prairie fire obscured the cursed mountains. His eyes grew blood-mad. "The One God tells us that we must be strong. The One God demands sacrifice."

"May we sacrifice our enemies."

"No. The One God demands that we sacrifice our own. The weak, those among us who cannot fight and destroy."

Nekena looked away. "The old?"

"Yes. They eat, but they do not fight. They make us weak. The young too; those who do not show strength and savagery."

"Children?"

"Yes, children. The weak among us must be sacrificed, in the shadow of this great temple. The God Stone commands it."

"Will He then stop the great fire?"

"Yes. We must do what our enemies refuse to do."

Twenty . . .

Thais spotted the small boy crouching in the bushes. He stared in disbelief; his eyes told that this was some kind of scout.

Thais stood still. He himself had been scouting up East Mountain, and hadn't expected to see anyone. Thais traded stares with the boy; they blinked their eyes at one another. This scout wore deer skin; many feathers flared out of his headband of leather. His face was the color of cedar wood. He was small and wiry; his eyes wanted peace.

Thais held his hands toward the boy's cautious eyes—a signal of friendship. The boy stood and walked out of the bushes, holding out his open hands. He stared down at the river valley, the caves of the Tolai. He was equipped with an atlatl, a brace of arrows, a hatchet and a stone knife. For his small size he looked capable; but he was not a Menkala.

Thais gave him a curious look. *You speak with the hands? Yes.*

You look hungry. Food?

Yes, I am hungry.

Where are you from?

The scout waved east. *Far out there in the flat lands.*

You are Paw-Nee?

Yes, the scout signed. *I am Paw-Nee.*

You are very young.

Look young, but not so young, signed the scout.

You are welcome here. You have traveled very far.

I crossed the land of the Menkala; I climbed these mountains. Many times I have risked my life. I am a great scout of the far Paw-Nee. We have heard songs of your people, and I am sent to make friends against the Menkala.

Thais studied this scout. His eyes grew wide watching the scout move, like a sinuous cat. He let out a grunt of astonishment.

You are a woman! He signed.

Yes. A hungry woman.

A Paw-Nee woman who has traveled from the east plains!

The scout smiled proudly. *A hungry and tired Paw-Nee woman who hopes to make friends with your people.*

Come with me. We will give you much food and rest. There is a wolf-woman who will want to meet you.

I have heard of the wolf-woman. The brave one who fights and hunts with men.

Her name is Mira. What is your name?

I am called Blue Bird. It was what my mother saw when I came into this world.

The Paw-Nee girl was welcomed into the Tolai village with much astonishment and curiosity. Mira made sure she was well fed and rested. Blue Bird slept long and ate well, and soon grew strong. She made quick friends with Shana, Wolf, Dona and the five puppies of the white wolf.

She watched Mira going about her daily duties. She studied these mountain people she had come so far and suffered so much to meet. She studied the wolf-girl of the songs.

I am not good at the hands, Mira signed. *I'm learning.*

Your name has come to me, Blue Bird signed. *A woman who hunts and fights like a man. A woman who fights the world.*

Do you not fight the world?

Yes, I fight the world.

Do you have a mate? Do you have children?

Blue Bird smiled sadly. *I have no one.*

You are a scout. Mira gave her an intense look. *You come from beyond the Short Hills. You have seen much of the world. You say that I am in songs; but it is you who should be in songs.*

Blue Bird smiled. *The gods decide who will be in songs.*

Why have you come to us?

We all fight the Menkala. Best to fight them together. A scout from these mountains, called Andar, has come to us. He has lived with us and learned our language. He speaks of uniting the enemies of the Menkala.

I will be honored to fight next to you, when the great and terrible thing comes.

Blue Bird smiled at Shana, covered in wriggling wolf puppies as the Hosho Dona smiled on. *You fought the demons,* she signed. *You fought those who have ever been enemies to us.*

My mate says that we must fight them or die.

This is true. But the way I fight them is to avoid them. They are monsters; and they would easily kill me in a fight.

There are many ways to fight, Mira signed. *What is your land like?*

It is wide and flat. Much grass, much sky. No mountains. It is a cruel land. We say that is what makes us strong.

I see that you are strong, Mira said with her hands. *How can you travel as you do—so far—and stay alive?*

Blue Bird smiled. *I watch the animals. They tell me what to do—and what not to.*

The Cold Days approach our mountains. You must stay with us until the warm days arrive. I want to learn so much from you! Will you stay with us when the mountain passes are closed with snow? Please stay!

I would like to—but I cannot. I need to tell my people that your people will fight with us.

Thais came into their cave; sat down cross-legged. Wolf puppies waddled up to him, and he rubbed them as they jumped on him, wanting to play.

"Look at these pups, Shana!" he said, laughing.

"That is Mama," Shana said. "That one is Daddy. That one is Turok. And Pretty. And the little one is Me."

"You gave them good names." Thais smiled at the Paw-Nee scout: *We all want the same thing,* he signed. *We only want to hunt the bison, that is all. For our families and our people.*

That is all we want, Blue Bird signed. *But you have heard of the God Stone.*

Yes. We would wish that *you stay with us until the spring. But if you must leave, let us send scouts with you.*

I will.

Mira touched her new friend on the arm: *How can a woman be a scout? How can a woman do what only men do?*

Blue Bird smiled and touched Mira's arm. *How can she not?*

Twenty-One . . .

Mira led her new Paw-Nee friend up East Mountain. They were both lean and muscular women, built like squirrels, and they delighted in scampering up the mountain, trying to out-do each other, laughing and pointing out plants of value. At the top of East Mountain Blue Bird pointed into the valley below.

Mira grinned. A bear was moving through the pine trees. They watched the great creature waddle across the rock and clay terrain.

Mira touched Blue Bird on the arm: *So many creatures walk the earth!* She signed.

Yes, I have seen them. You have seen them.

I have seen the great mammoths of the Short Hills.

I have seen them as well.

Do you have to leave so soon? Mira smiled. *Can you not stay through the cold days?*

Blue Bird smiled back. *I cannot. The snows will begin soon, and it is a great trek to my people. They will be anxious to hear of the mountain people who defeated the Menkala. Why do you cry, my friend?*

I am lonely. My best friend, Adela, was killed by the Menkala when they invaded our mountains. My mother has gone to the gods. Jella, the mate of Golthis lives away in the Conai caves; and a new friend I met of the Ooma is far away to the south.

We have sent scouts to them; it is important that all tribes who hunt the bison unite against the great monsters.

It cannot be that the gods made such a herd of shagbeards for only one tribe. They must be for all to hunt, even the wolves and lions and bears.

Even the hyenas, Blue Bird signed, frowning. *Those who make my stomach sick when they cackle.*

Whenever I meet a friend . . . Mira began crying again. *She always goes away.*

The Paw-Nee girl patted her on the arm. *You have so much. A beautiful daughter, a fine mate. You are known across the plains and deserts. My people, so far away, have made songs of you. They say if the girl of the wolf can fight and kill Menkala, they cannot be so frightening.*

But they are frightening.

Blue Bird stared eastward. She frowned. *They are human monsters.*

At the top of East Mountain, Blue Bird turned and signed: *Farewell, Mira.*

Mira, tears in her eyes, touched her fist to her heart. Blue Bird and her escort of five young Tolai warriors disappeared over the top of East Mountain. The warriors had been well-trained and instructed to carry valuable information across the Short Hills all the way to the beginning of the eastern prairie. They would winter with the Paw-Nee and bring information back to the mountains—if they survived. They knew that if they were captured they were to take the powder they carried in small bags on their necks—a powder Haldana had concocted that would cause instant death.

And they are being led, Thais thought, by a woman no older or bigger than Mira. He thought about the death powder of the shaman.

"Why you cry, Mama?"

Mira bent down and hugged Shana. "I made a friend and now she has to go home, that's all."

"Boo Bir showed me her hand sign words."

"She taught me too," Mira said. "She is the one who should be in the songs. She has courage far beyond me."

"She must be a tough and crafty one," Thais said. "I hope she gets herself and our men to the Paw-Nee. It's good that they have to go far south to skirt the black land of the western Short Hills."

"Where the great fire was."

"But I worry. The Menkala seem to be everywhere these days. The stone from the sky seems to be changing everything."

"These are terrible days, Thais!"

He gave her a grim look. "Not yet. And it seems we are making strong allies. The Paw-Nee are many, and very powerful."

"But they are so far away from us."

"Strange to say, that may be an advantage."

Thais had become obsessed with a great war plan. Could it be possible to attack the Menkala in the next season after this, on the Long Day, when the sun fell latest away, from three directions with different tribes: the Paw-Nee from the east, the Ooma from the south and the River Tribes from the west? If so, great preparations would be needed. The key to war is to make your enemy fight and kill himself. The enemy must give them time. In that time, would this new god make a stronger union between the Northern and Southern Menkala; or would they break apart and begin fighting again? Thais's biggest fear was that they would begin to spread and invade before a coalition could prepare, going after the Ooma first. To attack the Menkala in this way would mean very precise timing and much luck. But there might be other advantages to exploit: the scattered tribes of the north, the Chen and Crow and Pinor, had been creeping south to get at the bison herd. They were not united, but that could change. Thais knew little about them; only that they were thought to be weak, and they feared the Menkala, as any prudent people would. They had seen what he had seen many times: tribes burned to the ground, and the telltale staves of human skulls. Again his thoughts turned—not without shame—to thoughts of the poison Shaman Haldana made. Thais knew from his scouts the way it stood now with his old tribe; he suspected that his old friend Regga, now the High Priest of the God Stone, had probably poisoned both Xarran and Mogan Cariolus. Poison was considered the most cowardly weapon of all by the Menkala, a shameful insult to the gods. It might somehow make an advantage. Everything would have to be done to destroy the tribe of his birth.

Mira was gazing at East Mountain. What dangers and hardships and adventures has the woman scout of the Paw-Nee seen—Blue Bird? Would she have a mate and children one day?

"Blue Bird may fall in love with one of our scout escorts."

"It would be a good thing," Thais said.

"You cold, Mama?" Shana asked.

Mira was shivering. She prayed to the mountain gods that the Paw-Nee woman would find her way home. She wondered if she would ever see Blue Bird again, or Keal. She felt the coming of the prophecies, what everyone felt and no one dared speak of: the changing of the world. A great change sweeping over all tribes; a new god proclaimed to be the greatest god, one of savagery and war. A god come from the very sky to destroy them.

But if it had not been, Mira would not have had the adventures of her life: she would never have seen the Short Hills in the songs, the cave lions and short-faced bears, the dire wolves, the heart-stopping sight of the bison, the impossible sight of the great ones, the mammoths, who shuffled so slow and grey across the grass, the saber tooth cat skin that Thais had presented to her father when he asked to be her mate. She would never have beheld the demon tribe her mate had been born into. But no, that wasn't true. She would have seen the Menkala; she would have seen them as Adela saw them; demons pouring out of the trees, killing everyone, burning everything.

"One day, maybe you will see Lian again," she said to Shana.

"I want to, Mama."

Mira looked up at the top of East Mountain. "I pray to," she said.

"Can I see her tomorrow?"

Mira smiled. "Not tomorrow—but maybe someday, when the world is warm."

Twenty-Two . . .

"All unbelievers must be destroyed," Regga said. He gave Karas a meaningful look.

Karas made no expression. He knew how ruthless and dangerous Regga had become; he knew the meaning of the look. Regga ate the Mogan's magic each day now, and often his eyes burned with a madness.

"We rule our lands once again," Karas said. "Tribes no longer hunt the bison."

"Some still do," Nekana spoke up.

"The God Stone commands that now the Menkala must rule the world," said Regga.

Karas kept his eyes flat. He believed in the God Stone— he had seen it arrive at Earth—but he did not believe in Regga. A change had come over the man since he had become Mogan, the High Priest of the Menkala, as he now called himself. Xarran and Carilus were dead of some unknown disease. Now Regga with the new power of the God Stone. Regga, who was climbing skulls to be ruler of the world.

"The God Stone told you this?"

"Yes. The God Stone orders that we purify the world. Only when the world is purified of unbelievers will the

Menkala rule all. The mountains, the desert, the plains and the cold lands of the north. The God Stone tells me in visions that this is our destiny. We must not only keep them from the bison, we must own them; we must own their lands; their women, their children. The God Stone was sent to us so that we will own the world. All other gods have been destroyed, and any who still worship these gods must be destroyed. Menka commands that we purify the world. Slaves will feed us and keep us strong; it is given to the Menkala warriors to think only of war and the destruction of our enemies. The God Stone of Menka has revealed this to me in visions. Never have we ever been so powerful. Those who accept and worship the One God will be our slaves; those who refuse to abandon their old gods must be destroyed. In my dreams the God Stone commands this. Do you believe this, Karas, new chieftain?"

Karas nodded thoughtfully, mindful of how he had achieved the honor. "Ever we have worshipped the war god. We should begin with the River Tribes of the mountains."

"No. This is more important than vengeance against your brother," Regga said. "The God Stone has told me that you will have your revenge. But not this season; this season we must destroy the desert people in the south."

Nekena spoke up: "They are many, but they are weak. Not a race of warriors."

Karas looked at the Northern Menkala scout. Nekena had proven himself time and again as a superhuman, capable of running forever across the plains, of becoming a shadow; what the Menkala called Atta See (Death Shadow). He could appear to kill as a ghost, from bushes, boulders and grass. He could kill faster than a lion. He was the thing

116

that crouched in the darkness, invisible until you were dead. He ran among every horror of the plains, fearing none of them. Nekena could start fire quickly and scald any beast that approached him. The dire wolves knew his scent and stayed away from it. Nekena could count the human enemy and know what they had planned. He had used it against the Southern Menkala, his own cousins. Nekena could have killed Thais, and they would have been rid of a great danger. But Karas would not have that. Thais was his. Did Nekena suspect that Xarran and Carilus had been poisoned?

Karas feared that Regga would order Nekena to kill Thais, even though he promised not to. Karas distrusted Regga in these strange days—the days of the God Stone. With a weapon like Nekena at his command, Regga could read the enemies of the Menkala. Like Mogan Cariolus, Regga did not believe that Thais was the greatest enemy of his old tribe; Karas knew that he was.

He shocked Regga by asking the Northern Menkala scout, "What do you believe we should do?"

Nekena gave him a rat stare. "We must follow the commands of the God Stone. The mountain people would be very hard to destroy—you know this. The deserts to the south are flat. I can cross the Short Hills and enter the desert in three suns. The Ooma are many, but weak. If we destroy them, we can gain slaves and we can destroy an enemy that has united with your brother and the river tribes of the mountains. I believe the River Tribes will also unite with the Paw-Nee. Just two suns ago we attacked a scouting party far south. A Paw-Nee woman and five of the Tolai river tribe—the new tribe of your brother. They were trying to cross south of the Great Fire. They took poison and died before we could capture them. It can only be the River Tribes wanting to unite with the Paw-Nee. The woman was Paw-Nee. I think it was the one they call Blue Bird. Our enemies are uniting."

Regga frowned. "The God Stone says that this is true."

"If we destroy Thais, we destroy them. I know my brother."

"You make your brother more than he is," Nekena said. "I could have killed your brother twice."

Regga swept his hand across the air. "Thais is nothing! The God Stone tells me this. Your brother, Karas, is nothing compared to the warriors who will fight to death for the bison herd. The God Stone tells me that who rules the bison herd will rule the world. And only the believers in the One God, Menka, God of the Stone, will rule the bison herd; if we have the will and the courage, we will rule this earth."

"Ever the Menkala have had will and courage," Karas said. "The River People of the mountains—they do not worship the One God, they worship many gods. And Thais worships no gods. Why has the God Stone not destroyed them for their disbelief? Why has the God Stone allowed Thais and his spawn to live?" There, he had said it. The two men frowned at the question.

"It is not for any of us to question the God Stone," Nekena spoke up, flashing his bright eyes. "Regga, the Lord of the God Stone, speaks to Menka. I know this. Enemies must be destroyed—ever it has been this way—or they will destroy us. Your brother Thais knows this. He is a danger; but a weak danger. I could have killed him and been done with him."

Karas nodded to Nekena. "I know that. I do not question the God Stone."

"Do you question who the God Stone speaks to?" Regga demanded.

"No, I do not."

"I have scouted very far, into lands that do not yet belong to the Menkala," Nekena said. "Lands where the people fear the God Stone. The land is harsh and dry, but it is flat. The Ooma fight mostly with the rock sling. They prefer to stay away from warriors and to throw rocks at them."

"An easy people to destroy," Regga said.

"And for whatever reason, your brother formed an alliance with them," Nekena said "If we wait to attack the Ooma, Thais and his river people will come to their aid. If we attack them now, they will have no time to come to their aid."

"The Ooma are far away," Karas said. "Their land is without food and water."

"The God Stone tells me that they are an easy people to destroy," Regga said. "They dance back, and fight with slings."

"If we destroy the Ooma," Nekena said. "We may then destroy the Mountain People."

"The Tolai."

"The new people of your brother. The Giant, the woman of the Hosho Dona. If we attack the Ooma without hesitation, it will draw the mountain tribes down unprepared."

"I will do what the God Stone commands," Karas said.

Twenty-Three . . .

The Salotai reported that Menkala scouts were swarming over the land between the River Tribes and the Ooma, south in the desert. Thais knew that they were there to find a way to sever the link between the Mountain tribes and the Ooma. And that they would attack the Ooma in force and try to destroy them.

Thais met with Malek in a desert canyon between the two tribes. "I was afraid of this," he said.

"They have attacked us before," Malek said.

"Not like this. The Menkala no longer want to drive you away from the bison; they now want to destroy you."

"We will fight them to the death," Malek said.

"And we will fight them with you," Thais said. "But now there is a better way to fight them than to just fight them."

"What do you mean?"

"To retreat," Thais said. "To avoid fighting them; to retreat into your desert and make them follow you."

"To run away from them?"

"Yes! To run away from them. That is the last thing these Menkala want you to do. To draw them ever into the desert, where you can survive, and they can't. They want a battle, Malek—they Need a battle."

"The warriors of the Ooma will not run from any invader," Malek said.

"They must." Thais looked to the north, where Menkala were assembling; warriors that the Ooma warriors could not defeat. "Move south fast," he said. "The Menkala will chase you; then suddenly they will find themselves without food and water. The Mountain people are sending a force to fight with you, to menace the enemy from behind; but we are days away. It is now for you to avoid fighting the Menkala. Your people know how to live in this land, how to survive. The Menkala are a tribe of the plains, where food is everywhere. We of the Mountain People are coming to stand in war with you. Our hope is that you fall back into the desert and let our enemies weaken themselves. We are coming to fight with you. But you must not let the Menkala destroy you. Draw them deeper into the desert. Let them run out of food and supplies. Attack them with your slings; but then escape, and draw them deeper south. They have moved too quick against you. In order to win they must fight. In order to win you must not. We will attack them from the north, from the mountains. We might end this thing."

Malek looked at him: "We will retreat from them. But we will throw stones as we do."

Thais smiled. "May your stones cause them pain."

Twenty-Four . . .

The Menkala force, 500 strong, made camp along the river of the south desert. They were supreme warriors of the plains, but this was land that wore down the strongest of them. It was assumed that when they crossed the Grass River and invaded the lands of the Ooma the desert tribe would attack them and the battle of destruction would take place in this arid river valley. It was ideal fighting land for the Menkala; their plan was to push the Ooma back against mountains that rose across this river, giving them no chance to escape.

Karas, leader of the force, had opposed the invasion. Better, he thought, to assemble a much larger army and attack the Paw-Nee in the flat prairies to the east, where they had fought many times before; where food was plenty and land was known. But Nekena had reported the gathering forces of the Ooma at this desert river valley, and Regga, Lord of the God Stone, had ordered this quick and ill-advised campaign. Even now a force of the Mountain Tribes, 200 strong, was moving in to harass them from behind.

I knew they would do this, Karas thought.

The Ooma could be easily defeated here; but Karas's worst fear was coming to pass. The Ooma made campfires and a war dance and seemed to be preparing for an attack; but at dawn they were gone. They had retreated into the southern desert mountains.

"They run from us," Nekena said. "Now it is to chase them and cut them down."

"We would not be able to catch up to them," Karas said. He stared out at the desolate land to the south: dust and rock and cacti, and only stringy antelope to hunt. His warriors were exhausted from the long march south; every step in this desert weakened them; and though they believed that the God Stone would give them victory no matter where they went, no matter who they fought, Karas knew better. Before the God Stone he had prayed to the old gods of the Menkala, and many times They had failed him.

The God Stone could do anything; that meant that it could lie.

The strategy of the Ooma was to draw them ever southward, across dead mountains and into the even harsher deserts to the south. There the Ooma would not have to fight. The men had seen the abandoned camps of the Ooma, and their faces had grown from savage joy to grim exhaustion. They had already left a trail of their dead to the buzzards and hyenas. They would never speak it, but they knew in their hearts that the army must go back to the Short Hills or die. Many of these warriors had suffered defeat in the west mountains two seasons ago. Best to count losses and survive. Out there was only the land of death.

"We have conquered their lands and sent them running away," Nekena said, wanting to make a rabbit a bison; but Nekena knew the truth: the God Stone had not given them the promised battle; and out there in the desert they would die of thirst and hunger.

"We have conquered nothing," Karas said. "We cannot chase them into that desert. They know where water is, and we do not."

"This land belongs to us."

"Now it does," Karas said. "But it is one thing to conquer a land and another to keep it."

"Our men must fight," Nekena said. "Each night they pray to the God Stone for war. They have marched through all this hardship so that they could fight! How many have we left behind us—a trail of skeletons."

"There will be no one to fight if we go further, out there. The Ooma will keep retreating, knowing we march into death."

Nekena worshipped the God Stone; but he knew the truth. "It could be that the God Stone wishes that we turn north and destroy the mountain forces that attack from the north. They are led by your brother."

It was tempting bait, but he did not rise to it: "They will retreat into the mountains. Thais knows that we have weakened ourselves in this campaign against the Ooma. He knows that we haven't the strength to attack them."

"We have the God Stone!"

"My brother leads the Mountain warriors," Karas said. "He does not respect the God Stone. He knows that we cannot chase his forces into those mountains. He will let the mountains destroy us. Look at our warriors, Nekena! They pant from thirst and hunger. They grow weaker each day. Here at the fringe of the great desert they die in this heat and dust. We can defeat any enemy sent to fight us; but we cannot defeat the land."

"Your brother attacks our scouting parties, who move in the foothills. Do you not want to destroy Thais?"

Karas did not rise to the second bait: "That is my life, to take the life of my brother; but he knows this. We worship Menka, the great god of war. This gives us passion, this gives us fury. My brother seeks to use this passion and fury against us."

Nekena frowned. "I can go back and report to Regga."

"No. I will need you to scout Thais's warriors. Send others ahead." He did not want Nekena and Regga to fix blame to him. He had argued against this expedition; and it was no fault of his that the Ooma had refused to fight the decisive battle. These were times of distrust and intrigue. Regga now had the power of the people with him. Mogan Cariolus and Chieftain Xarran had died, he said to them, because they had sinned against the God Stone.

Karas knew: to return to the plains might mean his death. He had not come so far from the Flat River to retreat from the Ooma. But to pursue the Ooma would mean the death of his forces. He had faced defeat two seasons ago in the mountains, when his brother's army had attacked at night like shadows. Thais had defeated the Menkala by letting the hard world of the mountains weaken them. Karas knew that this was the same strategy. His warriors could not survive that desert, and they could not survive the mountains where, he knew, Thais would retreat to. His enemies could retreat; but the God Stone commanded no retreat for His warriors. Regga, holding court far north at the Flat River, crazed by a Mogan's magic herbs, would not forgive retreat. Nekena was here to ensure that the Ooma be destroyed.

Karas stared at the cruel south desert. He could not retreat; the God Stone commanded that he not retreat. He had brought warriors into this desert to destroy the Ooma, and destroy them he must. But how? His men could not survive on lizards and snakes. It was a dry dead world out there, without water. When his force was at its weakest, the Ooma would attack; and Thais would attack them from behind. He saw the strategy clearly in his mind. It was the same strategy Thais had used long ago, when in their childhood they had been pitted together by their father, to see who would triumph and who would fall. Always Thais had been the clever one, thinking far ahead, ignoring the gods. This strategy of the Ooma was the work of Thais—he knew this. To chase this desert tribe ever southward was certain destruction. He knew, deep in his heart, and what he could never speak: the power of Thais was that he did not believe gods existed

"They know that land out there," Karas said. "We do not. My scouts tell me that the mountain tribes are only a day behind us. They know we are growing weak, that we are out of food and water. Thais knows that we rule the Short Hills; but we do not rule this place."

"The High Priest Regga will not allow failure," Nekena said. "We have the power of the God Stone. Your brother does not worship the God Stone; he worships no god. Ever you have dreamed of destroying your brother, for his defiance of the God. If we place our lives in service to the One God, Menka, we cannot lose."

"We believe this—Thais does not." Karas saw the hand of his brother in this. To pursue the Ooma ever south into the desert was death. The God Stone had united the Menkala and made them once again masters of the plains, of the bison herd. But the God Stone could not protect them from reality.

"Thais knows that death waits for us out there," he said.

"Do you doubt the One God?" Nekena said. "Do you doubt the God Stone?"

"I know my brother. I know Thais."

"The Ooma run from us. It is only to chase them to death—"

"We cannot chase them to death." Karas stared out at the south desert. Sunlight glared on the dry desolate horizon, the stone mountains; the land where no food and no water existed. He did doubt the God Stone. The God Stone could not protect this army from what was out there—and Thais knew this.

Nekena sensed his mind: "Your brother is not far from us at this moment. My spies tell me that he is behind us, with a host of warriors. They wait to attack us. His mate is with him, the woman of the Hosho Dona."

"And his spawn," Karas said. "Who is called Shana."

"The High Priest Regga will not allow failure," Nekena said.

The High Priest. That title stuck in Karas's throat. He had known Regga since birth, when they were warrior apprentices, thrown into the world to kill or die. It was ever the Menkala way, to make brutal killers of their sons. Not Priests. He knew that his brother Thais was different; their father had said that Thais was the best of them because he was different.

"Have your scouts seen the Hosho Dona?"

"Yes. The white wolf is with them."

"The wolf who belongs to the mate of Thais."

"Yes. Mira." Nekena studied Karas. "Your brother cannot be so powerful if his first spawn was a female. The God Stone speaks to the High Priest Regga; the God Stone states that women are weak. The first born of Thais was a female. That shows that he is weak."

Karas again stared south, beyond the dry mountains. Death out there, for his warriors, for him. Death to go forward, death back on the plains; death for the stone that fell from the sky. Death to attack Thais and his crafty mountain warriors. He had never managed to defeat Thais.

"What do you think we should do, Nekena?" he asked.

Nekena's rat eyes danced over the dry desert. "To return without victory would be death," he said. "We came here to destroy the Ooma. They fear us; they flee from us."

"They flee, but they do not fear. Their plan is to draw us deeper into the desert, where they know we will grow weaker. We can conquer their lands; but they know that in time their lands will conquer us. And when we are at our weakest, they will attack."

"Then turn and destroy the mountain tribes, and have your revenge against your brother."

"The mountain tribes will do the same thing; they will run from us, into the mountains, wearing us down."

"You say that Thais once cried out that there are no gods. Thais angered the gods saying this. The One God will aid us in your brother's destruction."

"Gods have never aided in his destruction." Karas stared south at the desert.

Mira washed herself and then Shana at the river that twisted into the great desert of dust. Not far away were the fires of the Menkala army, sent to destroy the Ooma. In the distance she could see tiny figures against the dying sun, Menkala warriors; but she did not fear them. Thais assured her that they were exhausted, and many of them were falling dead from lack of water. Her own people were poised to disappear into the mountains if the Menkala turned to attack them. He believed they would make the fatal mistake of pursuing Keal's people further into the endless south deserts, where they could not hope to survive.

Mira did not like to see any living thing die; but she knew that it was the way of the world. Gazing out at the magnificent sunset, the far desert mountains of stone, she remembered a turtle she had killed next to the mountain river. She thought of the bison she had stabbed in a red fury, the mammoth cow she had climbed and stabbed in a great and glorious madness. The Menkala warriors who hesitated when they saw that she was a woman; and when they did how she had struck them without any thought of danger or death; with only an animal rage.

"We see Lian again, Mama?" Shana asked.

"No, My Papoose. Lian is going that way. We are going back to our mountains."

"Who are they, Mama?" Shana pointed to the Menkala scouts, the figures in the rocky distance.

"They are men who want to hurt us. But they will not. We will go back home, and they cannot follow us."

"Can they hurt Lian?"

"No, Love. Your friend goes with her mama into the far desert, where those men cannot follow. Lian is safe and we are safe."

"Why do they want to hurt us?"

"I don't know, My Papoose; I do not know. Don't fear, Shana. They will not come after us, because we have Dona."

Shana hugged the great white wolf that had come with them so far south of the mountains. "Will the puppies be all right without their mama?"

"Yes. They will be fine. And those men out there are afraid of Dona."

"How can they be afraid of Dona?"

"I cannot say, Shana. Your daddy said to bring her; and I think good Wolf is glad we did."

"Wolf loves Dona."

"Yes, he does."

Twenty-Five . . .

"I will die in the shadow of the Great Spire," Karas said. "But I will not destroy our warriors. If we try to pursue the Ooma the desert will destroy us; if we turn on Thais, the mountains will destroy us."

"The God Stone protects us," Nekena said. "If we retreat, we are defiling the One God; we will anger the God Stone."

"You know better." Karas stared south at the dry stone mountains, the merciless and endless deserts. "I saw with my unbelieving eyes the stone streak from the sky burning a tail of fire. At exactly the time that we were despairing the strength of our enemies. I do not doubt that this was a sign that we would regain the power of old."

"It has given us such power," Nekena said. "My scouts tell me the Ooma are already across those mountains, abandoning this land to us; and that the people of Thais are even now retreating into their mountains. They are weak; they are cowards. They fear the God Stone. They run away from us like rabbits! Look at the new lands we have won! Mogan Carilus proved this."

"We have won nothing. Dry dust and snakes." Karas looked bitterly westward, where the mountain warriors were escaping into their mountain strongholds.

"They run from us. They run from the God Stone. They are cowards."

"They do not run, they withdraw. And they are not cowards. My brother is an unbeliever, and I will hate him to my death. But he is no coward. He knows that sometimes to win, you run away."

"What will the High Priest say if we return to the Short Hills without victory?"

"I do not know. There was a time when Regga was a smart warrior. The God Stone has inflamed him with madness, as it did Mogan Cariolus. I am leader of this force, and I order that we return to the Short Hills, before we lose more men to this land. It will probably be that Regga orders my death. A great war awaits the Menkala; the God Stone inflames all tribes of the world. If we are to win this great war, it must be in our lands, where we have every advantage; where we have the bison."

"How can we retreat?"

"Our men are exhausted chasing the Ooma. They cannot survive the great mountains of the west. My brother knows this. And I know my brother; his strategy is to stand back and let us destroy ourselves. He may want to be of the peaceful mountain tribe, but he was born Menkala and he will always be Menkala."

"Let me kill him," Nekena said.

Karas stared at the great mountains. "Can you?"

"Yes! And I can kill his mate, and his child."

"The Hosho Dona protects them. I know that you can move like a shadow; it is said that you can appear as a ghost to attack undetected; but, Nekena, can you approach undetected under the protection of wolves? Even Thais, with all of his wiles, might not see you coming. Can you get past their wolves?"

Nekena frowned. He knew that he could not. "You are the leader, Karas. I will follow your orders."

"No warrior wants vengeance against Thais more than me; and no one has more right to demand it. But now is not the time."

Twenty-Six . . .

Mira returned home with the Tolai warriors from the Grass River. The Tolai village baked in warm mountain sun. The warriors were weary; many of them did not understand what had happened at the far Grass River. When they questioned Thais, he said, "We did not fight and we did not win. But we did not lose."

Shana sat with her puppies under the great aspen tree where Keane worked and measured the days with patient eyes.

"So, little mouse; again you saw the great desert."

"Yes, Keane," Shana said.

The old spear maker smiled at the child, awash in the spotted puppies of Dona. They wriggled over her as she hugged and petted them. The white wolf, Dona, stood with Mira's grey wolf.

"You've seen more than I ever have."

"We saw bad men, but Mama told me they would not hurt us, or Lian."

"Lian. Your Ooma friend."

Spring was over, and the hot summer sun blazed over the mountains. Keane had been busy with his young apprentices, making atlatls to be used in the great war that he knew was to come. Zianna, the witch of the Conai, had passed from the world; and he could feel that his own time was near. Despite the great struggles of men, he was beginning to see beyond, where spirits moved in the strange smoke of eternity. His was to spend the last energy arming his people and praying that they would prevail; that they would survive the changing of the world.

He smiled at Shana and the innocent puppies. He looked at Wolf and the Hosho Dona, who stood guard, staring at East Mountain as if they could sense the greatest thing that was to come. Keane had never believed that the weapons and tools he had spent his life creating would one day be used against men. He had heard the songs of the distant Short Hills and prairies; but these people—the Paw-Nee, the Ooma, the Crow People of the north, the savage Menkala—showed his mind the true size of the world, the true world beyond his familiar mountain home. He had once been a hunter, and he knew all of the mountains that surrounded the Tolai; he knew the deer and the elk and the white sheep that galloped down rocky slopes. He knew the many woods and stones and how they could be crafted into weapons and tools. He had lived many seasons, but he had never gone beyond these mountains. Here was a child, Shana, who had gone farther and seen more than he could imagine.

Well, it was in the misty hands of the gods. He could only take comfort in his craft. It was no longer wrong to make weapons that would be used against other men. He smiled at Shana, in the midst of the energetic puppies. Shana, child of war. So said the witch, who was now with the gods. His young students carved the willow arrows that warriors would use in the great war. Keane gazed west at the high mountains, still wearing snow. Now was a strange peace. The Tolai gathered food and made clothing from the mountain deer. He saw Mira wading in the river, her basket heavy with fish. No clouds drifted in the sky; there was only the bright yellow of the sun and blue quiet.

He smiled at Thais, who climbed up to Keane's familiar place under the aspen trees; the savage boy who had appeared to the Tolai and told them of the changing of the world.

"You smile, Keane," Thais said. "But it is a sad smile."

"I'm having dreams of the world beyond."

Thais frowned. "We all have those." He smiled at his daughter, playing with the wolf pups.

"I will probably not live to see the changing of the world—the changing of men."

"And women."

Keane stared out at the great mountains that he loved more than his life. "That is one of your strategies; is it not?"

"What?"

"I am no fool. I hear from the scouts and spies that travel to the Short Hills. I know the great weakness of our enemies as well as you."

"Tell me."

"Look out there, at the Tolai tribe. Look out at our people. At least half of them are women. The spies say that this new god of the Menkala degrades women. Women are weak, the new god says; women and girls must keep to themselves and only service men. They make slaves of those they conquer, and they make all women, even their own, slaves. That is their greatest weakness."

"They do not use half of their strength," Thais agreed. "I have seen the women of the Ooma, and how tough they are. I have seen the Paw-Nee scout Blue Bird brave what few men would brave; and I have seen little Mira in battle. The Menkala make their women slaves; and slaves will always fight against their slavery. If we allow our women to be warriors, they can make the difference. The Menkala believe that women are weak; but I see nothing weak about them."

Keane looked at Mira wading in the river, spearing fish with the girl spear he had made for her. "They are at least as strong as men. Will they help us destroy the Menkala?"

"Maybe. And maybe the death powder that Shaman Haldana can brew. I think that our enemies will destroy themselves, with help from us."

Keane fingered the atlatl arrow he was fashioning. "Why would they do that?"

"The Tolai love one another," Thais said. "The Menkala hate one another. We love life, they love death." Thais smiled seeing Shana playing with the puppies of the white wolf, Dona. He smiled at Mira fishing in the mountain river. He smiled at the warm sun and the quiet mountains. He smiled at Keane: "I believe that we will win because we are good, and they are evil. Maybe it is that simple."

Twenty-Seven . . .

Nekena came ahead of the returning Menkala army and met with High Priest Regga. "I do not believe Karas should die," he stated. "I agree with the decision of Karas to withdraw from the desert lands, where we would lose many warriors and gain nothing. Karas believes that we should fight our enemies here in our lands, and I agree. So, if Karas must die, then I should be killed as well."

Regga stared out of the magic fog of the god drugs he had eaten. Even so, his mind suspected a conspiracy. Nekena was a good comrade; a dangerous foe. Would the warriors despise Karas for his shameful retreat, or would they stand with him? These were crucial issues in these days of war. It was very bad that they had not destroyed the Ooma.

"What say our men?"

Nekena shrugged. "They did not want to pursue the Ooma further into the desert, though they protested the withdrawal."

"Karas did not attack the mountain tribes. There was no fight—no battle!"

"We could not have caught up to them. And the warriors fear the power of the white wolf."

"How can the power of the white wolf match the power of the God Stone?"

"I do not pretend to know these things," Nekena said. "Ever I have been a scout and a warrior. I know violence and death; I do not know what Menka wants of us. But Karas saved this army, I believe that."

Regga looked away. Nekena—a very dangerous man, one the Menkala called Tinga Tay (half-animal)—was too valuable to execute; it might break the unity with the Northern Menkala tribes. And Karas might have the loyalty of his warriors. The god drugs clouded Regga's mind. Often he retreated into the domain of stone under the great sandstone spear and stared at the black stone that Menka had sent from the world of gods. Menka ruled all of the gods so that Regga could rule the world of men. It was for this that he had poisoned Xarran and Mogan Cariolus.

"Can you go into the mountains and kill Thais?" he asked.

Nekena blinked his eyes in surprise. "It is possible. But Thais is a powerful man, with good weapons that he keeps with him. And a protection that even I cannot match."

"What is that?"

"Wolves. They protect the mountain people, and they warn them. Men I can kill, out of the darkness, out of the trees. Wolves I cannot. They have powers of detection beyond any man. They are faster than any man, and if a man is attacked without a weapon, the wolf will kill him."

"That is why the mountain people are befriending wolves."

"Yes. I have heard that the grey Wolf of Mira, the mate of Thais, has bred with the Hosho Dona. That will give them more of the beasts."

"I remember seeing the wolf of Mira in battle," Regga said. "How it astounded our warriors, how it went savage and attacked and tore the throats from them. I saw the mate of Thais spear two of our warriors in her fury; how they could not believe what they were seeing."

"That was in the mountains, their land," Nekena said. "Our warriors were bewitched by the mountains. Here we remain masters. Karas believes that is why we should let them come to us. The bison will bring them to us."

Regga blinked at the world, the hot summer sun. Around him women and slaves from conquered tribes worked to provide Menkala warriors with weapons and clothes. It was a society that operated on war. But all around him he felt deceit; eyes that were unsure; eyes that questioned the One God. In his god-state he felt enemies all around him. In his dreams he saw the wolves of the Mountain tribes; he saw the Hosho Dona.

Twenty-Eight . . .

"Keal and Lian are safe." Mira snuggled up to Thais and kissed his neck. "Those monsters did not follow the Ooma; they did not follow us."

"I wish they had," Thais said, stroking her hair. "My brother is smarter than I feared. Now they wait for us, because Karas knows that we must come to them, where they will have every advantage."

"Why can we not stay here, My Love? And live as we have always lived?"

"The bison," Thais said. "All speak of war and conquest and gods. Shamen and chieftains and warriors speak of the power of the gods. Tribes believe in God Stones and white wolves, they pray and worship the skies and the lands and the things that happen that cannot be explained. It is strange to say, but I believe that all that matters is the bison. In our times, in this world, it is the bison that will make power and strength. We can stay here and hunt the mountain deer and elk and sheep. But we cannot survive forever without that great herd that walks the Short Hills. All of the holy men speak of the changing of the world. The changing of the world is not the gods, or magic, or the ice of the north. For us, and for the Ooma, the Crow People of the north, the Paw-Nee of the east—it is the bison."

Mira climbed East Mountain to the white stone circle that enclosed the Place of Skeletons. She stood crying in the mild afternoon wind. The sweet smell of pine came from the high peaks of the west. She had seen the plains of the east, and the beautiful deserts of the south. She had never imagined that the lands of the earth could be so different. It all seemed impossible to her now, standing at this place where she had first met Thais; where now her mother and her stillborn child lay resting in eternity.

Mira fell to her knees and watched her tears fall to the dry ground.

"I miss you, Mama!" she cried. "I miss you so much! I miss you, My Baby! I miss you, My Turok!"

She thought of Turok; how the gods had taken him before he even tasted breath. She thought of little Coala, the chipmunk girl taken by the saber tooth; she thought of her brother Elat killed in the great Menkala battle. And she thought of her childhood friend Adela, murdered by the Menkala. She thought of Zianna, the Witch of the Conai, and how those ancient eyes were seeing beyond the sad world.

"I miss you, Mama. And I'm afraid. Terrible times are coming, and I know you want me to be brave. But I'm afraid, Mama! I'm afraid of this terrible war that everyone says is to come. I have dreams of the Short Hills. I see it in the eyes of the Shaman, and Keane, and Thais. Times are coming that will be terrible. I do not fear death for me— but I have Shana! I fear what the witch said about Shana.

All speak of this God Stone, and how a mighty and cruel god will now rule the world. All speak of Dona. The songs speak of me! I reap the magic herbs of the mountains, as you taught me. I brought home to Shaman the magic buttons of the cactus, where Keal wanders with her tribe. Never did I imagine, Mama, what world is out there; what wonders are beyond the mountains. It is beyond my mind.

"Now are quiet days. The winter is far away, and our hunters bring enough meat. Kem and Pak will survive the Cold Days, Shana will survive. Now it is mild, and the wind is sweet. My mate says that I should be happy, and to adore the life that is, while it lasts. I understand—but I fear what is beyond. You always were calm and wise, and the world seemed to make you a little sad. Keane makes me feel calm when he talks to me of the gods, and to love life before it is gone. But now Keane speaks of the other side, and how his dreams have shown him the mists that lay there. I have Thais; and I have Shana, who is more precious than me. You told me before you came here that life is only precious because it will one day be gone.

"I have seen many things, Mama. I have seen the great magic that is the world; I have seen great creatures that did not seem real, and wonders that I could never understand. I will see more, if I live, in the days that are to come—days of war. I do not fear death, I fear life.

"I miss you, Mama."

Twenty-Nine . . .

The Menkala force, under the command of Karas, returned to the Short Hills weak and demoralized. Many good warriors had been left dead on the hot plains and deserts of the south. Regga watched his men straggle into the main camp under the sandstone spear where the temple of the God Stone stood. Many of these Menkala warriors could barely walk. And he knew that a catastrophe had fallen upon his people. Even now the Northern Menkala were again quarreling with the Southern Menkala; none questioned the God Stone, but some questioned who should be its High Priest. And now all questioned who should be chieftain.

Nekena, ever the dangerous spy, appeared to him, in Regga's teepee under the Great Spire. Regga wondered if this man had formed a conspiracy with Karas, and if they would use this new disaster to destroy him. At the time of greatness, when all Menkala tribes were united, there came defeat at the hands of desert people who only threw rocks.

"How could these Ooma defeat us?" he demanded of the spy.

"They did not defeat us, they ran away from us." Nekena drank and ate and tried to regain his strength. It had been a terrible campaign that had cost the Menkala many men. "The desert defeated us."

"Why?"

"They fought us by not fighting us," Nekena said. "When they retreated from us, in the desert valley—when they went into the desert mountains—they were welcoming us into death. The enemy knew that we could not march farther from the Grass River. Karas knew better than to pursue them there. If he is to die for this, I should die too, because I believe he was right to withdraw."

"The God Stone does not permit the Menkala to run from our enemies," Regga said.

"Karas chose not to sacrifice an army," Nekena stated, staring away at nothing. "I believe he was right."

Regga frowned. He felt his power challenged; yet he was no fool. This disaster would shake the faith he had built up in his people: that they were the ones chosen by the One God to rule all; that they could not be defeated because the God Stone was theirs. Now the weak tribes of the desert had forced them back; and they feared entering the mountains to destroy the tribes of Thais. His people would see the staggering wretches that had been a mighty force he had ordered against their southern enemies. Slaves of the conquered tribes would see weakness; some would question the God Stone.

"Karas says that this is the work of his brother," Nekena said.

"Ever he has made his brother the main enemy."

"You know Thais as well as anyone. You are the ruler of the Menkala. What say you?"

Regga fixed him with a look: "Can you go into the mountains and kill Thais?"

"I could have before; now It would not be so easy. I think in these days he is very much on his guard."

Regga looked away. "The mountain tribes did not come this season to hunt the bison. We are still masters of the herd."

"I believe they will come, next season or after. They will come with an army." Nekena's sharp eyes stared out at the Short Hills, where the slaves of the Menkala labored to bring food to an army they no longer feared. Finally he ventured the question: "What will you do with Karas?"

Regga frowned. "Someone must pay for this disaster. Karas has sinned against the God Stone."

"He is a leader. He learned from his brother. He is too valuable to waste."

"I know his brother better than he. Thais is an unbeliever. But he is a very dangerous enemy."

"He makes the tribes of our enemies believe they can defeat us."

"That is why I want you to kill him. It should have been done long ago."

Nekena nodded. "What of his mate and his spawn? It is said in the songs that Mira killed two of our warriors in the great mountain fight."

"His first born is a daughter. The God Stone says that is a sign of weakness. But it is a very bad legend that this Mira truly killed Menkala warriors in battle."

"Songs tell of the Paw-Nee woman Blue Bird," Nekena said. "Yet she died when we found her. She did not fight us, she took poison."

Regga stared west, where the mountains rose into the sky. "There are too many legends," he said. "Rest here until you are strong; then go into the mountains and kill Thais, wolves or not. I will deal with Karas."

Thirty . . .

The wolves grumbled and looked up.

"Keep Wolf and Dona close to you," Thais whispered to Mira. "I must go into the mountains east."

She came awake from a deep sleep. "What?"

"I must leave for a little while. Go back to sleep. Keep Wolf and Dona close. I want it to seem that I'm with them."

Mira looked over at Shana, sleeping in her little bison blanket, snuggled up with the five puppies. She looked up at the cave entrance and her heart jumped: fifteen young warriors stood fully armed. Thais rose up from the ground and stood with them. "I must go, Mira; but I will return."

She was still sleep-dazed. "Go where? Why? No—come back to me. Why do you—"

Thais knelt down to kiss her cheek. "You must stay here and protect our child."

She looked at him. "I will stay here. But you must tell me."

"A Menkala has come to kill me. He will not approach me here because of Wolf and Dona. So I must go to him."

"No!"

"Listen, Love," Thais whispered into her ear. "You must stay here, and you must keep Wolf and Dona close. This

Menkala will take his final chance, and with luck I will kill him. He has been following us ever since we went to the Ooma last season. I think I know who he is. I believe I can kill him, though he is a good killer."

Mira looked out of the cave mouth at the full moon behind the stern Tolai warriors. "Is Shana in danger?"

"We are all in danger, My Love. We have always been in danger. He has not crept in to kill me because he fears the wolves. So keep Wolf and Dona here and close to you. Keep your spear with you in case. Wolf and Dona will attack anyone who approaches to hurt you and Shana and the pups. The killer knows this."

Mira looked at the young warriors. "This killer is not alone."

Thais smiled. "My little warrior. No, he is not. It is the time to see if the mountain warriors can be like cougars. I believe they can."

"This killer—"

"He is very good, Mira. But I believe I am better."

"I know that you are better."

"Keep the wolves close, My Love. I will return soon."

Thais knew that the Menkala killer was behind him, panting in the thin mountain air. Thais found a nest in the boulders, and there he quickly stuffed a bison hide with grass, placing the form in a crouching position, so that the half-moon faintly illuminated it. Then he crept into a mass of boulders on East Mountain and became a shadow. The young Tolai warriors were very good, and would use their mountain lungs and complete knowledge of this valley as he had trained them. But these were Menkala warriors, and he knew how they had been trained since birth. Now it was to see if the young Tolai men he had trained could truly be like cougars, and could kill great warriors without hesitating. They outnumbered Nekena's braves three-to-one. He knew that they had heard of the God Stone that fell from Heaven; and that they feared its magic power. He had trained them to put no ideas of fear into their minds when it came time to act, and he was confident that they would kill without fear. Keane had given them the best weapons, and they were young men with strong muscles, strong instincts, and anger that their homes were being invaded. They knew well the fate of other tribes, whose staved warriors stood white-skulled in the light of the moon, whose mothers and daughters and children lay dead and headless in red ashes.

Thais saw a flicker of movement, and sooner than he expected it happened. Nekena leaped out of the dark and attacked the straw-filled form. Nekena stabbed savagely, and knew immediately that it was not Thais. He rolled away from the form; then jerked as an atlatl arrow shot into his back. It was a shocking pain, and Nekena scrabbled like a speared cat, clawing the arrow out. He crawled desperately toward the shadows of a bush. Another arrow came with a *whoosh!* and crippled him. Nekena knew that he was dead. He hadn't the strength to pull the second arrow out. He lay panting in the dark, gripping his knife. He could not sense his companions around him; he could sense nothing.

Thais dropped down from his hiding place, squatting near him, like a panther, but not near enough to attack. Nekena tried to tear out the second arrow, but the pain was too great. He felt a strange poison coursing through him. He had used poisoned arrows himself, and he knew that these were poisoned. He lay back on the mountain soil, knowing that his end had finally come.

"Thais," he said. "Do se min atta (you bring me death)."

"Speak river tongue," Thais said. "I know you can."

Nekena stared at the milky shadows. The moon glowed overhead, brightened and darkened as clouds passed over its face. "I am not alone," he said.

"Yes, you are. I brought men too. They were well trained, and they know this valley in the dark, every bit of it. You brought five and I brought fifteen."

"And their arrows are poisoned."

"Yes."

"And your arrows are poisoned."

"Yes."

"The same poison your men and the young woman took when we found them trying to cross our lands to get to the Paw-Nee."

Thais stared at him. "Blue Bird," he said.

"A brave woman, like your mate."

"There is more than poison in your veins. There is poison throughout the land."

Nekena nodded and stared up at the clouded moon. He could feel the poison in his blood; he could feel life clawing out of his body. Yet it was a strangely comforting sensation. Many times in his life he had tried to imagine death. Now it was here. "You have sent me to the gods, Thais."

"It is said that, for the Menkala, there is now only one god."

"I do not know these things. It could be I only pretended to. Like you, I know the world. I do not know the beyond."

Thais watched him, still the panther. Nekena lay back and felt his own energy flow out, like slow water. "I cannot attack you," he said. "You have killed me, you can relax."

"Non septa o so kalla (no rest for the warriors)," said Thais.

"I rest now. After a life of war, now I rest."

"You are the one they call Nekena. Of the Northern Menkala."

"Yes. I know you more than you know."

"I know you also. I have been aware of you for a long time."

"I could have killed you." Nekena smiled, but he felt his mind growing numb. The poison of the arrows took away the pain; he could no longer move. He stared at the moon, at the clouds passing over these mountains.

"My brother would not let you," Thais said.

"He would not."

"So Regga sent you to kill me."

"Yes."

"I knew Regga from childhood. He was ever wanting to rule the world."

"That is his dream now. The God Stone has made a madness in him. He is no longer a Menkala warrior; now he is Mogan." Nekena fought to get his breath. Too much talking here at the end. He lay staring at the moon.

"We could have lived in peace, the Menkala and the Tolai," Thais said. "We could have shared the bison. We could have grown strong together."

Nekena panted out the last of his breath. "Essa co Menkala, Thais (you are Menkala, Thais). You call yourself something else, but you will always be Menkala. I do not know the answer . . . you do not . . ."

Thais watched the man die, Nekena's eyes finally seeing beyond the clouded moon. It was a silent night; no wind moved in this mountain valley. Fragrant shrubs scented the air, the plants that Mira harvested and mixed with her bison stew. Thais stared into the night. He thought of Mira. He thought of Shana. The killer Nekana was right: He did not know the answer.

Thirty-One . . .

Karas arrived at the camp of Regga a haggard man, near death. The army of warriors he had led south could barely walk, their eyes on the ground, their strength spent. Slaves watched them march in like walking dead. The Menkala had conquered many tribes in the last two seasons; slaves worked the Short Hills, warriors were eager to die for the God Stone. Yet a spirit of ruin seemed to come, as a slow storm, growing black on the horizon. Regga's mind was fogged; he had eaten the magic and it had made a dark magic. He prayed to the one God, Menka; the cold God, the hard God; God of conquest, of pain and death.

He looked at Karas, broken and defeated, who had always been defeated by his brother. Karas sat cross-legged in the Great Teepee of the Great Priest, the Mogan. Karas looked down to the ground.

"Kill me," Karas said to the ground. "We could never have defeated the Ooma because we could never have defeated their land."

"Menka has spoken to me," said Regga. "He forgives your failure, and so I forgive your failure. Ever have you been a great warrior, a leader of men. Menka commands that you be spared, to grow strong and to fight again."

Karas stared at the ground. The god Menka had commanded the expedition against the Ooma, saying that it could not fail. Karas knew Regga's strategy: to spare his life at the expense of blaming him for the debacle in the south desert. If the One God could do anything, the One God could lie. Karas had returned here wanting to die. He still did not know if he wanted life; he was too wasted to know. His mind did not care; but his body longed for food and rest. Regga was sparing him because Regga needed him; the great war that was building needed a commander who could move armies, who knew better than the new Mogan who no longer had the trust of the people. He understood that Regga wanted to kill him, but could not. Regga needed his support. The warriors that had survived the desert knew that Regga had sent them to certain death and Karas had saved them, as many as he could. Regga had the power of the God Stone, but Karas had the power of the army. The Menkala united north and south were still the most powerful force of the plains. But tribes beyond the plains were uniting. He knew that Regga had become power-mad, and would make decisions that would lead to destruction. The Paw-Nee woman found on the southern plains with Tolai warriors—those who took poison before they could be tortured—would be in the songs of the enemy. Menkala women were mere slaves who, in these days of the God Stone, dared not even speak. The Paw-Nee woman had died with her Mountain escorts. But torture or not, Karas knew that it meant that the Mountain People were trying to form a union with the far tribes of the plains.

He looked up from the ground. "Where is Nekena?" he asked.

"I sent Nekena into the west mountains to kill your brother."

Karas nodded and looked once again at the ground. "As the God Stone commanded."

"Yes, as the God Stone commanded. I know you claimed Thais as your trophy; Thais and his mate, the wolf girl, and their spawn. The God Stone has spoken against this. The God Stone commands that you live only to rebuild the armies of the Menkala, that they can fight the world and conquer the world and burn the world. In my god-dreams I see our enemies dead—skulls on spears—their camps burnt to ash. The One God, Menka, commands that we destroy all others so that we rule the world."

"What if Nekena fails?"

"Nekena carries the power of the God Stone." Regga's eyes were dazed, drunk on power that he could not control. "How can you question the God Menka?"

"I do not question Him," Karas said. "But I know my brother."

"I know your brother better than you. Thais chose weakness over strength. He chose a disgraceful life over an honorable death. Your brother angers the God Stone; he cannot survive the power of the One God."

"Thais did not choose weakness. He does not believe in Menka; he does not believe in the gods. The One God has not destroyed him, and I do not think Nekena will. Kill me if you must, Regga. But you know that the great war is coming. I told you long ago that my brother must be destroyed. Now he tries to unite many tribes against us. Tales fly across the world, of Thais, of his mate, the wolf-girl, of the giant of the south, Golthis; the giant with one eye and an ax that will fell a dozen warriors. Tales now begin of the Paw-Nee girl Blue Bird, and her courage."

"She is dead. She took poison when we captured her. She was a mere woman. This Blue Bird is dead."

Karas looked at the ground. "Is she?"

Thirty-Two . . .

Malek led the army of Ooma hunters north into the land where the great bison herd watered at Grass River. Malek's legendary feats and courage had made him a leader as respected among his people as Thais was with the Tolai. This was a dangerous move, returning his people north and invading the lands of the Southern Menkala; but he had reasons for doing it: a great harvest of bison in the hot days of summer would give his people food and strength to face the war that was to come. And he wanted his men to feel that they could enter the lands of the Menkala as the enemy had entered the desert. He wanted them to march across a path that was littered with Menkala dead, those dreaded warriors led by the war lord Karas, the enemies who had died of thirst and heat. He wanted them to see the corpses, and to know that they could defeat the monsters of the north who claimed the bison for themselves.

The Ooma hunters marched past the bodies of dead Menkala, and when they crossed the Grass River and approached the bison herd, a party of warriors appeared on a mesa and gave hand signs. They were young warriors from the Salotai tribe of the tall mountains. Malek went up to the mesa to speak to them. The leader of the Salotai warriors gave messages from Thais: of a meeting in the Autumn Sun, just before the Cold Days; to plan on the great war; to attack the Menkala on the Long Day next season. The mountain tribes would move from the west, the Ooma from the south. With luck the Paw-Nee would attack from the east. Thais had even sent brave young Tolai north to meet with the scattered tribes across the river. Malek had only heard of them in legend: Crow people and Tribes of the Bear; people who came from their frozen world to take of the great bison herd.

"I have only heard of these people in old songs," Malek said. "I have heard that the Menkala have burned many of their villages and taken many slaves."

"This is true," the young Salotai warrior said.

Malek stared away. "Do they have fear in their hearts?"

"I do not know. But I believe that it is as Thais told me: in these times, in these days, there can be no fear."

"Not even of the God Stone?"

"That is the god of the Menkala. It is not our god."

"We will meet on the Autumn Day," Malek said.

"At the great river of the desert. When the Cold Days have passed there will be the war. We pray that Paw-Nee will be there, and that those of the north tribes will be there. These are the times that will be in songs long after we have passed. Thais wanted me to tell you this: ever he will be your friend. Ever he will fight with your people. This great war for the bison will decide the fate of all of our people. Gods will not fight this war. We must fight this war."

Malek studied the Salotai warrior. "You are very young."

"I am sixteen seasons."

"Young but very fierce. What is your name?"

"I am called Andar."

"You are too young for a mate." Malek smiled fondly at him. "Will you and your scouts come to our camp and be fed? I would like my hunters to see the courage of the mountain people. How they raise their young with such bravery."

"With pleasure," Andar said. He looked at the force of Ooma scattered along the river valley. "I know that we will defeat the Menkala, so that all tribes can have the buffalo."

"How do you know this?"

"When I saw my little sister train to be a warrior."

Thirty-Three . . .

"Soon we will see Keal and Lian again, My Papoose." Mira stroked Shana's long brown hair. Wolf puppies scampered around them as they sat near the river. A cool breeze blew from the west. Above, under the aspens, Keane and his apprentices made weapons as always. Thais was in the tall mountains with hunters, stalking the deer and elk and the white sheep. Her father, Etain, sat speaking with Shaman Haldana; she knew they were speaking of things to come. The early autumn day was mild and beautiful, the aspens shimmering gold in the wind; Mira knew that this would not last. She felt the great growling of the earth, of dark things gathering, of gods stirring the peace into terrible war. Tribes beyond the sun were preparing; the monsters of the Short Hills were preparing, those beings who were born for war. Watching her little girl play with the wolf puppies, Mira could not understand evil. She knew of evil, she had seen it. But she could not understand it. Seeing the wolf puppies galloping in the sunshine, she could not understand evil.

The Menkala lived to destroy. She had heard tales of what had happened to the tribes of the north; how Menkala had murdered them and taken them as slaves and burned their camps to the ground. Such horror went beyond her mind. She did not fear death. She no longer feared the gods. It was only now to live through the Cold Days and then when the Long Sun appeared in the sky, to go into war without fear. She had asked Thais how this ever came to be, and he had told her that it was always meant to be.

"I want to take a puppy to Lian," Shana said.

Mira smiled. "On the Autumn Day, when we visit the Ooma, you can take one of the puppies to Lian. Which one?"

"Turok."

"He is a good pup. He will grow into a great wolf, and he will protect Lian. The Autumn Day grows near; then we will be off on another adventure. Do you like adventure, Papoose?"

"I'm not sure, Mama. But I want to see Lian."

"I want to see Keal. And maybe we will eat snake again. I liked it."

Shana giggled. "And we take Turok. Will Dona miss him?"

Mira petted her daughter's hair. "A mother will always miss her child. But she must let her pup go into the world; that is the way of things. And Lian will love Turok and care for him, and he will grow into a mighty wolf, and he will protect her. Dona will have more puppies, and the world will go on."

"Will Grandpa go to the adventure with us, Mama?"

Mira looked at her father, sitting in council with Haldana. "I think not, Shana. He is weary, and he misses your grandmama. He is a great chieftain, but he is finally tired. He gives the future to the young, as Wolf and Dona give the future to these puppies. See how they jump and scamper, how they are in love with life; how they grow strong and show their courage even before they are grown?"

"I miss Grandmama."

"I do too." Mira held back tears. She stared at the sky, where lazy clouds moved slow in the wind. The sweetness of the mountains came to her, the pine scent and the fresh smell of the river. The blessings of the gods. "When we go on our adventure, Papoose," she said. "We will take all of the wolf pups. One we will give to our friends of the Conai, and one to the Emotai and one to the Salotai; but Turok we will save to give to Lian."

"Will Wolf and Dona go on the adventure with us?"

"Yes, they will. And you must stay close to them always. They will protect you if your daddy and I cannot."

"From the bad men who want to hurt us, Mama."

Mira cried, and held her daughter. "That is true, My Papoose. There are bad men out there, and they want to hurt us. I will never lie to you. Out there the world is dangerous; I wish it were not."

Mira watched her daughter wrestle with the wolf pups, the fierce babies who would grow into great wolves. She thought of the Menkala, there on the Short Hills; those who believed that only they could have the bison herd, that they ruled the world, that they ruled others. Demons that enslaved their women. Mira felt the white hate that had come to her seasons ago, when she faced down such demons, with their devil tattoos and their cruel muscles. How they stared at her when in her red madness she had stabbed them with the girl spear Keane had given to her.

How brave was the Paw-Nee scout Blue Bird, traveling across the plains.

"What did your daddy say to you, Shana? On this adventure to the Ooma on the Autumn Day—what did he say to you?"

"He said that courage is the only thing."

Thirty-Four . . .

A week before the Autumn Day they set out for the southern desert. Wolf and Dona and the five wolf pups made their way into the adventure, watching closely after Shana. She loved to sleep with the pups, and with Dona alert like a white statue. Wolf followed Thais and the young scouts into the mountains, but there seemed to be no Menkala following them this time. When they reached the Conai camp Golthis the giant joined them and said that there was an uprising in the Short Hills.

"The slaves they made are finally turning on them," he said to Thais. "It took them long enough."

Thais slapped him on the back. "I have heard that you are the new chieftain of the Conai," he said. "Now you can eat to your heart's content."

"No. Jella keeps my eating down. She is heavy with another child. She says that in the war that is to come the army will not need a fat giant. My spies tell me that the Paw-Nee girl and your men were found by the Menkala, and they are dead."

"I think that is true." Thais frowned. "These are dangerous times, my friend. With another child on the way, should you be going with us far to the Ooma camp?"

"Jella says that if I don't go, she will make my life miserable." Golthis bellowed out a laugh. "I see worry on your brow, Thais. But together we will kill the enemy and make our songs. I have seen you fight. You have seen me fight. Damn the gods, I say! Believe what you will; I have never seen a god fight."

Thais smiled. "Do you want a son or a daughter?"

"I want a daughter. Sons are too much trouble."

"Shana brings a wolf pup to your children."

Golthis gave an ugly eye to the distance. "Yes, I know. They are creatures I am beginning to respect."

"When we scout, we keep an eye on Mira's Wolf. No man can approach us in secret when Wolf is with us. Remember when I told you that wolves will one day more than pay their way?"

"They are turning out to be good weapons." Golthis smiled at the south. "When we destroy your old people, we will have the bison; we will hunt the giant mammoths together; and one day I will fight a lion."

"They are not easy to fight," Thais said. "The Menkala are not easy to fight. But we are lucky that the Menkala are ever destroying themselves. We make friends and they make enemies. We trust and they deceive. I would give my life for you, Golthis. The Menkala do not understand the friendship that we feel. That is one of their great weaknesses."

"I know that their slaves are finally fighting back," Golthis said. "In the war that is to come one of the Menkala may spear me dead; but not before I crush his head with my ax. I have seen my children grow strong on the bison steaks; I have seen them sleeping on warm bison beds; I have seen my tribe grow strong on the meat of the bison. I will fight the demons who say we cannot hunt the bison. I believe the snake people down there feel the same."

Thais smiled. "And the far Paw-Nee. These are times, my friend, that make our lives. I am glad to be in the world with you, in these times."

Golthis smashed him on the back. "We will fight and we will win. By my one good eye, we will make songs beyond our lives! I long for this war, and to fight those who kill and make slaves. If there are gods, if there are no gods, I want to fight those who would kill my children."

"I am ashamed of those who raised me," Thais said. "I was raised to fight and to die. But now I have Mira, and I have Shana."

"Children make a difference," Golthis agreed. "They are all really that we leave behind."

Mira sat with Jella by the river. Their children waded in the water and played with Dona's wolf puppies. It was a mild day. Clouds drifted over the mountains in the pine wind. Mira patted Jella's belly and smiled. "You will bring another joy into the world. In these times of war, you will bring joy."

"And so will you. One day, Mira, you will not bleed in the time of the moon, and you will bring a joy into the world." Jella looked to the east. "There is great evil out there, I hear. My fool of a man aches to fight this evil. He talks in his sleep of fighting and killing Menkala, and he almost smothers me."

Mira laughed with Jella. "Thais talks in his sleep of the same fighting."

"I think you do also, Mira."

167

"I wish it were not so. I wish the world could always be as it is now; a world of sun and children and puppies splashing in the river. I wonder what the women of the Menkala are like."

"It is said that they live like slaves, and cannot be with the men except . . . well . . . what does Thais say of them?"

"He had no sister; and he will not speak of his mother. He only says that the Menkala do not respect women, and that makes them weak."

"It would do me no good to try and make you stay here, while the men go back to that desert, so I won't try. You are in songs, and ever you have craved adventure, Mira. But the witch said that you have the power of the white wolf. I am with child, or I would go on this adventure with you. I would like to see Keal and her children."

"I will ask her to travel back with us from the desert," Mira said.

"May she travel here with her people," Jella said. "And we will have a celebration for them. My big and ugly mate is now chieftain, so I can order a feast. Bring Keal to us; bring Lian. I believe that the people of the south desert are good people."

"I hope that one day we can go there together with our children. I have my mate and my child; but I am lonely; I have no friends who live close. I wish you were close, I wish Keal was close; I wish Blue Bird of the Paw-Nee was close, so that I could talk to her. I love you all, but you live in tribes far from me. In these times of war, I feel lonely."

Jella hugged her. "I am always close, Mira. I believe that you have great courage and great fear. I do not know what the world will bring to us in these times. I saw with you the great land of the bison. I carved them with you, and we hanged their flesh to dry in the wind. We still have the dried meat of those beasts; they feed my children and they feed me. I sleep with my man on their warm blankets. I believe your friend Keal sleeps on the bison. I saw in the Short Hills that these beasts go beyond the eyes. You will go back to the people of the south desert, and my mate will go with you. They will plan war when the Cold Days have passed. I accept this. I pray to the gods, but they tell me nothing, Mira."

"Yours is only to bring the joy into this world that is in your belly. Be it a boy or a girl, you must only bring it into this world."

Jella was looking at her. "You will not let Shana stay here with us."

"No. Shana must go with me. She must see the world. Wolf will protect her."

"And the white wolf."

"It is said that the Menkala fear a white wolf."

Jella looked at Dona, the white wolf, standing guard over the children, over her pups. "Golthis tells me at night that a great war is brewing. He holds me when I shiver at this thought. He tells me that he will be in the songs; that he will kill those who want to kill me, and our children. I am proud of him. By all the gods, Mira, I am proud of him!"

"As you should be." Mira smiled and patted Jella's stomach.

Thirty-Five . . .

Again they marched into the great desert of the south, and Mira saw something that went beyond her eyes. It was a giant ball of armor plates, similar to the desert boulders; but this moved on stubby legs, and it had a face!

"Do you see it down there, Mate?"

"I see it." Thais watched the creature move slowly across the desert sand.

"Do you see it, Shana?"

"Yes, Mama. What is it?"

"I do not know."

"Nor do I," Thais said. "I've never seen such a creature."

Wolf and Dona approached the moving boulder, and suddenly it retracted itself, becoming a living rock. The dogs sniffed at it, then cocked their heads at one another.

"It has armor against enemies," Thais said. "Maybe Malek or Keal will explain what this is."

"Such a land!" Mira said. "Such a world. Come here, you two!" she called to the wolves. "That creature may be poison."

"It is the strangest creature I've ever seen," said Thais. "Golthis, come look at this thing."

The giant lumbered up and stared down into the desert valley. "Why do the wolves sniff at that rock?"

"It is no rock," Mira said. "It is a creature, an animal of armor."

"By the gods." Golthis shook his head. "Snakes and lizards creep across this dry land; but never could I believe something like that. We should capture it and take it back home. It would be forever in the songs."

"It seems peaceful," Thais said. "It does not bother us."

"Wolf! Dona! Come here and leave it alone!" Mira called.

"It is a huge creature," Golthis said.

"It seems to be a giant of its kind," said Thais. "Like you. You should respect that."

"I do." Golthis grinned at the distance. "Over this dry mesa we see again the people of the snakes. They may tell of this creature. Jella will not believe me when I tell of this monster of armor. But you're right, we should leave it in peace."

A day later Mira hugged Keal and Shana hugged Lian and gave her the spotted puppy Turok. The Ooma gathered round them in a great crowd and whispered like rippling wind. They stared, but not at any of the mountain people; they stared at Dona, the pure white wolf. They made signs with their hands against their bodies, and Mira heard what must be prayers muttered. Dona looked at them with tense curiosity. Wolf, not liking the great crowd around them, stood at her side and grumbled.

"The Hosho Dona," Thais said.

Malek pushed them through the throng, yelling out stern orders that Mira could not understand. Soon the excitement was spent, and the feast resumed.

The Ooma had returned from the Short Hills with much bison. Their enemies, the Menkala, lay dead from thirst. Malek smashed Golthis on the back and the giant grinned.

"Do your men learn the skills of the slings?" he asked.

"They do," Golthis said. The giant looked out over the great desert, at spiked cactuses and dry sand, and the mild rainbow of sunset that painted the western skies. He was a legend to these people; he was in their songs. "The slings are great weapons, I cannot deny that. We prepare with you for the great war that will say whether we can have the bison or not. My mate tells me that I yearn to fight, to prove my strength; this is true. I yearn to fight those monsters up there. May the gods forgive me, I Want to fight them!"

"And be in the songs." Malek smiled. "I cannot deny that I want to fight. It should not be—but it is. We gather here to prepare for war; I cannot deny that my heart longs for war. It is maybe against the wishes of the gods, I do not know these things."

"Nor do I," said Golthis. "But our children grow strong on the meat of the bison. Our children, the boys and the girls, grow strong because we have courage, and we teach them courage. It is said that the Menkala make slaves of their women; Thais says that this makes them weak, and I believe that. My mate, Jella, is heavy with child. She is a woman, and she is stronger than any man I've met."

Malek smiled. "My mate, Keal, is the same. She tells me that she wants to fight in the great war, alongside Mira, the mate of Thais. Keal wants to be in the songs. My mate uses the sling as no warrior I have ever seen."

Golthis grinned. He was very drunk on the cactus. "I do not fear the enemy; I do not fear the Menkala. I will smash them with my ax when the time comes. My mate is called Jella, and she brings to me another child. If there is anyone I fear, it is her."

Thirty-Six . . .

The Autumn Day came, and the Ooma gave a great celebration for the River tribes. There was joy in the air, but also fear. Only a day ago an Ooma boy had gone into the bushes to relieve himself, and dire wolves had taken him. The giant wolves, attracted to cooking meat, shadowed the camp. Shana had seen a great shadow away in the valley, and Thais said that it was a sabertooth. When celebrations took place and meat was cooked there were always great predators just beyond the campfires.

Mira sat with Keal and the Ooma women. Their children took turns playing with the new puppy Turok. The weather was warm, but when the sun set it reminded all of the Cold Days. Giggles went round when Mira was presented with a bowl of the magic cactus juice. Mira drank, knowing her mind would grow warm and joyful.

After the Cold Days, Mira, Keal signed. *I will go to war with you. And I will be in the songs.*

Mira smiled and patted her on the arm. *I am so glad to see you again. See how our daughters play? On this Autumn Day my heart is calm.*

She told Keal of the creature they had seen in the desert, the giant thing of armor. *It was like nothing I could imagine!*

It is good that you left it alone. It is a sacred creature to our people. It only eats bugs, and it does not trouble the world.

This is a vast and wonderful place, Mira signed. She drank the cactus juice, and she smiled at the desert. Shana and Lian scampered up from the river and got dried off. Turok the puppy danced and barked at the bonfire that was set in the middle of the feast. Wolf stood with Dona and they watched the feast, and they sniffed at tame coyotes who ventured up to them to make friends. Mira felt that the world was perfect; but then Keal grabbed her hand.

Men of your tribe come, she signed.

Mira saw the young Salotai Andar come into the camp, with warriors of the mountains. Thais spoke with them, Golthis towering over the conference. Malek nodded grimly, and the men retired to the teepee of the Ooma shaman.

Keal touched her on the arm. *That warrior is so young.*

He is already in songs. He brings news of our enemies.

I want to be in songs, as you are.

Mira drank down the cup of cactus, and the Ooma women refilled it. *I love you, Keal. Will you come to our lands? My friend, Jella, who is mate to the Giant Golthis, wants to meet you. She is with child, or she would be here.*

Yes. My mate has traveled far and wide; now I will travel with him to your lands. Together we will be in the songs!

Mira watched the warriors retire to talk. *When the Cold Days are over, there will be war, Keal. I am afraid of what is coming. Is it not enough that the wolves and the knife-tooth threaten our children?*

You are the woman of the white wolf, Keal signed. *I want to be like you. I want to see what you have seen. I want to see your mountains and to meet your people. I long to be in the songs. I want to be in adventures.*

Do you ever get lonely?

Yes, I do, Keal signed. *Are you ever afraid, Mira?*

Mira drank down the bowl of the cactus juice. Keal filled it back up.

Yes; I am often afraid. For my child, for my people. Being in songs does not mean being unafraid.

We are much alike, Mira. Though we live in far-away tribes.

Mira drank of the cactus, her mind growing comfortable and strangely sad. *I fear the Cold Days.*

See the women of the Ooma? How they watch you?

They laugh to see me get drunk on this juice.

No. They watch you because you do Not have fear. You say you have fear . . . but no. Keal smiled and touched her heart with a fist.

Mira smiled and touched her heart with a fist.

Thirty-Seven . . .

"It must happen on the Long Day," Thais said. "We have much time to prepare; but we will be fighting Menkala on their land." He looked at the young Salotai scout Andar, who challenged everything and feared nothing. "This young man has gone across the wide plains and met with the Paw-Nee. He has even learned to speak Paw-Nee."

Golthis sized him up. "You are a young one."

"I will be seventeen seasons soon," said Andar. "One day I hope to be in the songs as the Giant of the South is."

Golthis smiled in spite of himself. Then he made an ugly, drunken fist: "These Menkala paint themselves to make fear; they make themselves ugly in order to make fear. They want you to be afraid! To see their tattoos and take your eyes off their spears!"

"I know they do," Andar said.

"But they die like any man," Thais said.

"True." Golthis took a great drink of his cactus juice. "They take an eye or a leg, but by the gods, I have seen them die!"

The men at the conference all laughed. Then the Ooma shaman cleared his throat and they grew respectfully silent.

"Our chieftain is Malek So Conya," he said. "Let him now speak."

"I have been in the lands of the Menkala, Thais's old tribe," Malek spoke up. "They are the enemy, and they must be defeated if we are to harvest the bison. As Golthis says, they are at war with their slaves, and with themselves. But when they are attacked they will be savage fighters. We meet here to say that when the Cold Days have passed and when the day of the Long Sun arrives, we all must be in position to attack. We know that there can be no retreat as there was this summer when they came into Ooma lands to destroy us. We did not defeat them, our desert did—I know this. When the Long Sun arrives, there can only be attack and destroy. We have the Cold Days to prepare for this." He looked at the young Salotai. "The Paw-Nee; will they attack from the east?"

"They will," Andar said. "They ache to fight with us."

The Shaman looked at Thais. "These are your people we speak of fighting. What say you?"

"It will not be easy," Thais said. "The Short Hills of the plains is their land; they will fight to the death any force that invades. And they will fight to the death for their new god. They are fast and fierce killers, and they have been raised from birth to kill. Your tribe are hunters; my tribe, the Tolai, are hunters. But hunters are not warriors. We have time to train, and we have advantages that we must use in order to win. We have defeated the Menkala, and you have defeated them; but it was in our own lands, not theirs. Menkala are trained to fight close; we must fight from afar; with slings and atlatls—and poison."

The Ooma Shaman gave him a look of pure shock: "Poison?"

"Yes. You know of what I speak," Thais said. He gave Malek his own dark look. "Train your men with the atlatl; make the arrows sharp and coat them with the poison of the snake that rattles. The snake that lives all over this desert. There is more poison in this desert than any army can use. That is a great weapon. You know how to do this."

"Yes, we do," Malek said. "This is poison only used against the animals we hunt."

"That is what we will be doing when the Long Sun arrives," Thais said. "We will be hunting animals—the most dangerous of all. The poison of the desert snake that rattles may give us victory."

"Our gods may forbid this," the shaman said.

"If they do," Thais said. "Then we may not win. We must invade and attack, if we ever are to rid ourselves of the Menkala and share the bison. But the Menkala will destroy us very quick, if we do not use every advantage we can have. Slings thrown by strong and accurate arms. Warriors who learn the most important lesson—when to back away from the fight, let the enemy come to him weaker. And how to use poison." He glanced at Golthis. "You do not agree."

"No. But you're giving a good speech."

"We must train like demons during the Cold Days," Thais said. "We must give our warriors such skills that they believe they can win, that they must win; and finally, that they will win."

"I must consult the gods," the Ooma shaman muttered.

The young warrior Andar spoke up, surprising all: "Gods will not fight this war. We must fight this war."

"Well said, young one." Golthis smashed him on the back.

"We will use poison," Malek said. "We will use every advantage against the enemy. I see the strategy that Thais says: We do not fight the enemy his way; we fight our way. We fight with our stones and slings, and we fight with poison."

"I know that this is troubling to all," Thais said. "But there is nothing more for it: we will be going into a terrible war against a terrible army. We must not believe that the Menkala will be easy to defeat; they will not. They have weaknesses that we must exploit. We have time to weaken them in the Cold Days. The far Paw-Nee know of our plans, and I believe that on the Long Sun they will attack. There are tribes north of the Great Flat River that have been burned by the Menkala; many of them are now slaves longing for revenge. This must be a greater war than any of us have ever known. The Menkala know that we are uniting for it; and they are uniting for it. I wish that this would never have come to be—but it is. We must fight them together as friends."

"This is not about gods," Andar spoke up, turning heads.

Thais smiled at him. "This young warrior speaks the truth. This is about the great bison herd. It is the life blood of all our tribes. It is enough to make all of our people strong, to make our children strong. We fight and hope to make a great song; or we wither away like cowards."

"There can be no crying and moaning about this," Golthis spoke up. "I will fight next to the Ooma, the

Paw-Nee and those of the north. Or I will fight by myself. I will fight for those bison."

"What of the God Stone?" asked the shaman.

"I do not fear a stone from the sky," Golthis said.

"And you, young man." The shaman looked at Andar. "Do you not fear the gods?"

"I do not," Andar said. "My tribe, the Salotai of the mountains, will fight and they will die. I have been to the Short Hills, and I have beheld our enemies. I am young, but I am strong. I have no fear of this tribe that wants to keep us from the bison hunt. I have only hate for them."

"I wish you were my son." Golthis smiled at him.

"So it is agreed," Malek said. "Our people spend the Cold Days preparing for this great war. And on the day of the Long Sun, we take our lives to the enemy, together."

"Together," Thais said. "And there is another weapon that might take the heart of the Menkala."

"What is that?" asked the shaman.

"My mate, Mira, tells me that there are many Ooma young girls and women who want to train to fight."

A silence fell, but only for a few moments until Golthis spoke up: "If they want to fight, let them fight."

"Every advantage." Malek smiled at Thais. "Your mate has inspired them. We will train our women to fight alongside the men."

"I must consult the gods," the Ooma shaman said, staring down.

"Of course," Thais said. "One other important weapon: I see many tame dogs in your camp."

"Dogs?" Malek looked at him.

"I know that dogs can be trained for war. And they are a great weapon. You fight to the death, and they will fight to the death with you. If our tribes can invade the Short Hills and fight the Menkala, may they have dogs with them. The Menkala despise dogs, coyotes or wolves. They kill the mother and wipe out her den of pups—because the wolves are doing what we are doing: hunting the bison. What they don't know, and what I have come to see, is that when they destroy the pups they are destroying a great weapon, and a great gift."

"Understood," Malek said.

Thirty-Eight . . .

Weeks later, when they had returned home, Shana stared out of the cave. She knelt down to pet Dona, who rubbed against her. "See the clouds, Mama?" she asked.

Mira came to her and looked out at the west, where black clouds were forming over the far high peaks. "The Cold Days begin, Papoose," she said. "There will be snow. And I feel the wind picking up."

"A storm, Mama?"

"Yes, a storm is coming. It looks like much snow. It will get cold, so you sleep close to Dona."

"And you sleep with Wolf. I think they miss the puppies."

Mira smiled. "I will."

"Why is the boy Andar staying with us?"

Mira gave her daughter a startled look. "He speaks to your daddy. He speaks of things to come."

"War?"

Mira frowned. She thought of the Witch of the Conai and what she had said. "Yes. There will be war. But first there will be a storm."

Together they sat and watched the dark clouds rush in. Down below in the river valley the Tolai scampered to prepare for snow and wind. Keane hobbled up to his cave to start his fire; Shaman Haldana and Etain came up to the caves, wrapping their bison robes around old shoulders. Thais and the hunters galloped up from the river as the wind whipped down from the peaks. Mira had seen this many times, the sudden icy fury of the gods. She felt the wind rush down from the west; and now silvery mists of snow sparkled and flew.

Mira stirred the bison stew that bubbled over their cave fire. "Your Dasha is going to be hungry. And it is going to be one of those nights."

"Can we gather at the counsel fire and listen to the songs and stories?" Shana asked.

"Yes, we will, after we eat."

"I like the new songs you sing of Boo Bir from east."

"I do too, Love. And tomorrow, if it is not too cold, we can go out and scoop up snow and make honey-balls. Then you invite your friends to our cave for treats."

"I don't like the Cold Days," Shana said.

"They come so that we rejoice at the Warm Days." She was reminded of what her mother Odele often said to her: "Good times are only precious because there are bad times."

"I like the snow," Shana said.

"It is beautiful when it makes the valley clean and white. The Cold Days will come; this must be. But then the Warm Days will come, and the great god of the sun will smile again."

"What do the gods look like, Mama?"

"I cannot say. They show us their powers, in the wind and sun and snow, in the river. But they do not show us their faces, or their forms."

"How do we know they're real?"

"How can they not be real?"

"I hear Shaman talk about Dona," Shana said. "I hear him talk about a witch."

"The Witch of Conai." Mira stared away.

"Who is she?"

"A friend. A wise friend."

"Did she have to go home, like Boo Bir?"

"Yes, Papoose; she had to go home."

Thirty-Nine . . .

"You are beyond your years," Thais said to the young Salotai warrior. They walked through the snow along the river. The mountains had turned cold and hard, but there was no wind. The snow lay blinding white in the bright winter sun. Thais patted the young man on the back, wishing that he was a son. "It is dangerous to be beyond your years," he warned him.

Andar gazed at East Mountain. "It is because of songs I heard about you. I want to learn from you—how to fight, how to have courage. The great tale of my tribe is the one of Thais going alone into those mountains and killing a knifetooth."

"I killed it by out-smarting it; by using its hunger against it. Here is your most important weapon." Thais tapped his head.

"Yes; and also what you saw in the desert." Andar smiled. "I saw it too."

"Show me."

Andar removed a home-made sling from his belt and fed a smooth oval stone into its pouch. "A very easy weapon to make; and stones are everywhere. It takes much practice to learn, but it may be the key to our victory on the Long

Sun. That tree there. Will you stand here and throw an arrow at it?"

Thais loaded an arrow into his atlatl and shot it; the arrow stuck into the tree and it shivered for a moment. "Be warned, Andar: the Menkala are taught to do this in their sleep."

"And to kill close up with a spear."

"Yes."

"Now I will shoot at the tree."

Thais watched as the young man backed away at least thirty paces beyond where he had launched the arrow. Andar's muscular arm whipped the sling round and sent the stone flying at the tree. Thais was stunned at the sound of the impact, the stone sending hard bark flying. Both warriors approached the tree and Thais touched a great scar the stone had made. "I saw what the Ooma did to cactus," he said. "But this bark is as hard as a man's skull."

"Can any of our people match the spears of the Menkala?"

"No."

"Do the Menkala know the true power of this simple weapon that can be made by any warrior in a day?"

"No." Thais grinned at the young man. "They say it is a woman's weapon. No Menkala warrior would dare use or carry a sling. But today you have shown me what a weapon it is. Good atlatl arrows are hard to make; and spears even more difficult."

"But stones are everywhere."

"This must be our goal," Thais said. "We all must train hard with these, at least as backup weapons."

"They are very light and easy to make. But it took me much time and training to master it."

"You have great courage, Andar. And wisdom far beyond your years. But know this: great courage brings great danger. And in these times, there is great danger."

"I know danger. I am not afraid of danger."

"When I was of your age I knew danger; it was not so long ago. I never feared death. I never feared danger; I worshipped it." Thais gave him an intense look. His breath came out like a white ghost: "Never tell anyone this: I never worshipped any gods, but I always worshipped danger."

"When I heard songs of you," Andar said. "I knew that you challenged the world. And I wanted to challenge the world."

"That is a dangerous thing." Thais looked away at the mountains. "But maybe it is the only thing."

"I stay with your tribe through the Cold Days," Andar said. "Other warriors of my tribe are there to teach skills that will be needed. I have come to know the wise men of your tribe, Keane and Etain and Haldana. But they are old, and they cannot fight this war with us."

"I am glad you are here; you are a young but very inspiring warrior. This will be needed in the times of the great war. All tribes who are the enemies of the Menkala know that on the day of the Long Sun, war must come. It will be a terrible thing, I fear; and I wish it had never come. I would like to live in this river valley forever in peace, with my child and my mate and maybe children to come. I wish that my life could have come to that."

"But it did not," Andar said.

"No, it did not. Maybe the instant I ran from my tribe, the Menkala, I knew that my life would be one of war. The Witch of the Conai told me this. You have heard tales of her."

"I saw her," Andar said. "I was only young, and knew nothing; but she looked at me with strange eyes that I will never forget."

"She must have seen a great warrior. Did she speak to you?"

"No." Andar stared away at the mountains. "But she looked at me."

Forty . . .

"How many did the slaves kill?" Regga said, his eyes grim and hard.

"They have been slaughtered," said Karas. "Our slaves paint the snow red."

"How many!"

"Fifty of our warriors, or so. They attacked us because we returned weak from the desert. They found weapons, and they waited for the Cold Days to attack. It was madness. We destroyed many of them."

"How did they find weapons?"

"Weapons are everywhere, if you need to find them."

"Fifty great Menkala warriors! In the shadow of the great war!"

"We tore them from the earth," Karas said. "This uprising is destroyed, and no slaves will dare ever attack us again."

"Fifty dead." Regga stared up at the great spear of sandstone, at the temple on the plains. A frigid wind blew like death from the western mountains. His eyes were glazed. Out there in the Short Hills the slaves of the Menkala lay, carnage for the lions and hyenas, wolves bears and coyotes.

"How can our enemies fear us if even our slaves do not fear us?"

Karas also looked out at the desolate winter. "What of Nekena? Has he returned? Did he kill my brother?"

"No word from Nekena. He has not returned from the mountains; his men have not returned."

"I did not think they would." Karas sighed. "Now it is only for us to prepare for the great war when winter ends. Our enemies gather against us, I know this. The Ooma, the River Tribes, the Paw-Nee; even, I fear, the tribes of the north. When they learn that even our slaves attack us, they will take courage."

"No force can defeat the Menkala," Regga said. "The God Stone has given us power beyond any tribe. Slaves fought us and we destroyed them."

"Slaves fought us. They fought us hopelessly with clubs and stones. Can it be that we have angered Menka? Can we have sinned?"

"The purification of the world will not be easy. Tribes have had their gods before any memory. Many will die before they will believe; and so die they must."

Karas looked at Regga, seeing the change in his face, his eyes. Regga would often retire into the new temple to eat Shaman's magic; often he fell into spells of mumbling words that could not be understood. The words of Menka, the believers said. Regga was growing gaunt and grey before his years, and often he stumbled when he walked. He seemed almost a haunted figure. He never left the sight of the Spearhead that formed a landmark on the endless prairie. In the far west were the smudges on the horizon of the great mountains, where Menkala raiders had met so much grief. Karas sensed a doom in this cold winter day. The God Stone had united the Northern and Southern Menkala; but it also united the enemies. Karas did not know of gods or their plans. But he knew that even gods could not keep the tribes of men from the great bison herd. It was too vast to patrol. His people could make slaves hunt for them and feed them as they trained for war; but Karas sensed that this was a road to eventual ruin. Ever the Menkala had hunted the bison and fought the dangers of the earth. But this stone he had seen with his eyes ride the tail of fire from Heaven had changed all. Now there was talk of purifying the world. It was not enough to fire the Menkala with the new religion, the One God: now all others must bow to Menka. Karas believed this; but he no longer believed in Regga, and in the dark of night his mind went to thoughts of murder.

Regga stared at him with piercing eyes. "You were gone with the warriors when your brother gained his manhood; I was his best friend. You think you know him? You think you know his mind? I know the great power Thais will try to bring against us, against the God Stone. Yes, he brings warriors and weapons; but he is far more clever than you know. Thais will bring against us a weapon more powerful than any we have ever faced. It is not men or armies, your brother knows this. It is a danger that he sows that may destroy us if we do not destroy it."

"What is it?" Karas asked.

"It is freedom. Believe in the God Stone, and one day Thais will kneel to you."

Karas stared out at the mountains. He was willing to believe in the One God that he had seen come from the sky; but one thing he could not believe: that Thais would ever kneel to anyone.

Forty-One . . .

Andar spent the Cold Days with Chieftain Etain in his cave next to the cave of Mira and Thais. Outside was the large cave space of the family. Kem had his own tiny cave space, and Pak had hers, but often nightmares would send her into Mira's cave. The Tolai liked privacy, but in those prehistoric times the first North Americans still lived close and by necessity watched closely over one another. Each night during the Cold Days the tribe gathered in the Great Cave below Mira's. She would climb down an incline and enter a huge space around which several other small alcoves, hung with hide doors, marked the personal caves of Haldana, Keane and many others. The Tolai, in the days far beyond memory had been a nomadic tribe before settling in this protected and fortunate honeycomb of caves that rose above the clear, fresh river.

Etain was grateful for the company and support of the young Salotai warrior: his broken leg had never completely healed, and now old age was beginning to pain him. Mira gave him herbs from the mountains to ease the pain, but a life of hard work and battle—with animals and men—had finally taken its toll. Andar watched out for him and helped him negotiate the earth ramp that led down to the great cave where a bonfire blazed each night during the Cold Days and the songs and stories of the Tolai were told. Also, Etain welcomed the company. His family had moved out, one by one, his wife had died. Like Haldana and Keane, Etain was beginning to see visions of the other side, where the gods lived.

Andar, for his part, was proud to spend time with Etain and Thais. The caves of the Salotai were not as large as those of the Tolai, and having three sisters and two brothers, he had never enjoyed this much space. Each day he would wander down into the cold wind and snow to teach the Tolai warriors, many of them girls, what he had learned of the sling. Stones sailed hissing across the snow to tear into tree targets as the Tolai tried to out-do one another. All mountain tribes were training their men and women for war, a new generation who waded the snow to their targets with grim, determined faces, their eyes seeing tattooed monsters, their minds on the future and the great war that was to come after the Cold Days. Older tribe members, mothers and fathers who had lived in peace and security all their lives, gathered and looked down from their caves with worried faces, seeing the new generation prepare to fight and kill other people. Ever their gods had commanded peace; and now to gather armies and weapons, to become warriors. Even girls and women . . . these were indeed times of great worry and dread. Worse, their children would not be fighting here in the familiar mountains, but out there on the distant plains. They knew that when the Long Day approached and they said farewell to the armies, some would never see their sons and daughters again.

But the young warriors from all tribes—the Tolai, Conai, the Emotai and Salotai—young women and men of the Ooma, the Paw-nee and the tribes of the north, could feel the new future that was dawning on their lives, and they embraced it with a fierce and murderous passion. They were already considering themselves the Children of the Bison. Tools, clothes, weapons, food, all forms of decorations and sacred skulls had come from the bison and made them strong. Those who had traveled to the Short Hills and hunted the giant beasts knew that a day of hunting there would bring a hundred times the meat and treasures as a month of hunting deer and elk in the mountains. They would fight for their people and their families and their mountains; and they were willing to fight to the death for the bison.

Thais, Mira, Shana and a small host of Tolai warriors followed Andar south down the river to hold council with the three tribes along the way. The way was cold and brittle, the snow dry on the ground; but the west mountains blocked the wind, and there was only the sound of crunching feet. Golthis met them at the Conai camp and a feast was prepared. He had been blessed with a new daughter, and Mira couldn't wait to take Shana up to his mountain cave to see the baby. Jella was tired, but happy.

"This is getting tiresome," she said. "Giving birth to children too big for my body. This child stretched me like a deer hide."

"She is beautiful," Mira said, holding the baby in its tiny bison robe. "What is her name?"

"Tinia," Jella said. "We named her after my mother."

"Isn't she pretty, Shana?"

"Hello, Tinia," Shana said. "See the world? It's pretty."

Jella smiled at her. "This one grows like a pine tree."

Mira's eyes grew tears as she rocked the new baby in her arms. "I wish I could have another. We try; but still I bleed."

"It could be that the gods are saving you for war. If the Menkala fear any of us, it is probably you and your wolves." Jella stared into space. "Never has my life been ruled by such fear. How could the world have come to this?"

"I cannot answer that, my friend. Maybe no one can. It is all part of the changing of the world."

"I shouldn't speak like this in front of Shana."

"I always tell Shana the way it is," said Mira. "So does her father. One day she may have to fight."

"And this one." Jella shuddered looking at her new baby. "Golthis tells me that our tribe would not have survived the world as we were, bison or not."

"I believe that is true. The Menkala were planning against us before we ever went into the Short Hills." Now Mira stared away. "They would have come to destroy us. I know not how the gods could let such things happen, how they did not protect us in our peace. Nightly I ask my mother what the gods ask of us; I ask the Witch of your tribe; I ask all who have gone to the gods. I have even sneaked some of Haldana's magic herbs into my mouth to find out."

"Mira . . . you didn't!" Jella looked down at Shana, who was calmly cooing at the baby Tinia. "How could you do this?"

"To know," Mira said. "But I was told nothing—I saw nothing from beyond, or from the gods. These things are maybe not for us to know."

"Often I would see the witch making signs at the sky, speaking to the gods. Did she not tell you anything of why this came to be?"

"I don't think even she knew."

"I have brought another child into the world!" Golthis bellowed, punching Andar on the back and nearly knocking him over. The giant's mouth breathed steam into the still air, and smelled of bison meat. "Let that be a lesson to you to push out your seed when you can. You're never too young when you first get the urge. I have brought another child into the world, Thais!"

"I think it might have been Jella who brought Tinia into the world." Thais studied the Conai warriors practicing slings and atlatls down near the river. "You have more women than we do," he observed.

"Conai women grow contrary, and believe they can do as well as men."

"I believe they can." Thais admired the sling-work of the Conai. He had entered the Cold Days very fearful of what was to come: if the tribes of the mountains were sending their young into a slaughter that would destroy them all. For if the river tribes were destroyed by the Menkala, the Menkala would come into these mountains to destroy all that remained. It was to be a war of survival this time, nothing less. A war out there in the lands of his youth against the tribes of his youth. But seeing the young, and how they responded to his many trainings and teachings, his heart lifted. They had courage and hate; they were quickly developing skills, and fighting together in a way that astounded him. He had not seen a shadow of fear in any of them.

"One day—young warrior," Golthis said to Andar. "If you survive, that is; one day you will have your chance to be in songs. It might be your last and only chance."

"If the gods will it, one day I will be in songs, as you are. I will do my best."

"If you happen to be at my side when the storm hits, you had better." Golthis glared down with his one fearsome eye at the young warrior, who knew he was already in plenty of fire songs and tales.

Thais smiled. The giant knew that young Andar stood in awe of him, and he was playing it for all it was worth. "One thing I want to discuss," Thais said. "A strategy that is terrible. Speak nothing of what I tell you—but think about it: it would be a deed more terrible among the Menklala than any there ever was. It is a great sin even in these mountains. It is something that the Menkala would probably never suspect."

Andar and Golthis were watching him. "Go on," Golthis said.

"Last summer the Short Hills were very dry; not enough rain. This season the plains may also be very dry, even drier. It may be what my people called 'Zehasa', the Dryness. Sometimes the Dryness goes for many seasons, and ever it has tormented the Menkala. You saw what happened last season."

"The great fire," Andar said. "I saw it many times in the distance when I was scouting." He looked at Thais. "You are thinking of using such fire against our enemies."

Thais shrugged. "If the right time comes, and the grass is dry and the wind is blowing toward them."

The three men were silent. "To purposely set a wild fire," Andar murmured, staring at Thais. "Even in war . . ."

"It is the greatest crime and the greatest sin known to the Menkala." Thais looked at Golthis. "A sin more awful than any against the gods, war or not."

"Hm." Golthis was thoughtful for a moment. "It doesn't seem to stop them from burning Our land. One of my sisters, of the Palotai, died in the fires those devils set."

"I want you to think about it," Thais said. "At the right place and time, it could be an army greater than any we can field. The flames of a prairie fire, if the wind is blowing hard, would send terror into our enemies and send them running for their lives, and would kill many many of them."

Andar was blinking his eyes; he was worried about this, but a spark of revelation was glinting.

Forty-Two . . .

Etain and Keane sat in the cave of Shaman Haldana and the three men passed the pipe of the spearhead plant. They had been friends for many seasons, and many times had smoked the spearhead plant and spoken their thoughts and feelings and visions. In these times, change had come upon them like a winter storm; only not to savage the land, but life itself. Momentarily they would speak of these things; but now they were three old friends, and they spent a few moments discussing their ailments:

"My hands are getting to where I can no longer make an atlatl," Keane started it off by grumbling.

"The leg I had broken," Etain said. "It is beginning to fail me. On rough terrain Andar has to help me not to fall down," he confessed.

"I have seen the young man holding you up when you come down the ramp to the Great Hall."

"And I have seen your youngsters fashioning the tools and weapons while you sit under the aspen and tell them how poor are their skills."

Keane smiled. "A life of work deserves some rest. And they are poor in their skills." He accepted the spearhead pipe from Haldana, who had taken a deep breath of it. The shaman blew the grey smoke into the cave and stared at his modest fire.

"You have your bodies to complain of," he said. "I fear that it is my mind that is failing. I forget things. Things I have known all my life—I am forgetting them."

"I am forgetting many things." Etain took the pipe from Keane.

"Maybe it is that the gods give old men forgetfulness in order to give them peace."

Keane blew smoke into the air. "I forget tools many times. I have to press my mind to remember the right tool. My hands are too painful and cramped to use them; some of the apprentices look at me in worry; then I have to yell at them."

"Had I not broken this leg," Etain said. "I would have tried to go to the Long Days war. That would have been the way I would have died; like my son."

"Elat will live forever in the songs of the Tolai," said Haldana. "And songs are coming that will forget the songs of our youth. The three of us—old men now—often spoke of the changing of the world. How each year the river is not the same; how the mountains are not the same. But the old must always give the coming days to the young."

Keane nodded sadly at the fire. "When our young go off to fight, this will be a very lonely place." He frowned at what he said, and glanced at Etain, who was the only one with children.

But Etain merely nodded sadly. "I wish I could be there with him."

"We are old, the three of us," Haldana said. "But we have all given our strength to this thing: I have made great amounts of poison for Thais; Keane, you are making them fine weapons. Etain, you are filling their hearts with courage and pride."

"It angers me that I tire so quickly," Keane growled. "Often I want to just lie in the shade and smoke the spearhead plant and just dream."

"You lay in the shade already, old friend." Etain smiled.

"And you walk attached to that young blond Salotai."

"I too am having trouble walking," Haldana said. "I grow dizzy and I stumble. We, of course, are all having dreams of the beyond."

"My wife Odele told me of dreams she had before she died; I know she spoke of them to you, Shaman."

"Yes."

"She told them to me as well," Keane said. "Of a peaceful and beautiful place she did not want to awake from."

"We have all been honorable men, who gave our lives to the tribe," Etain said. "The gods will favor us; I know this. May we smoke the spearhead plant beyond, just like this."

The three of them stared into the fire and were silent for a while as they passed the pipe. Shadows flickered in the shaman's cave, blinking like yellow eyes at the paintings in reds and browns and whites. Of hunters, mountain elk, of the pure white sheep of the high peaks; of sacred totems and the births of babies; of the bison, and yellow and red war—finally the painting that seemed to dominate the rock wall—the white wolf.

"This God Stone of the Menkala that comes to us in tales," Keane broke the silence. "Could it have been as the streaks of fire that we see every night? Could those also be stones the gods are throwing down on us? You are the holy man. Can it be that there is only one god?"

"I have prayed for the answer, since the tale of the God Stone reached my ears. I have thought long about it; and I can only say that there are either many gods, each with a power, or one god with many powers."

"It is not for us to know these things," Etain said. "Maybe we will know when we drift into the beyond. I do not fear it; I believe that I will see Odele in the beyond."

"I no longer fear it," Keane said.

"Nor I," said Haldana. "Ever I have been the tribe's holy man—and I cannot know. I hope that death will let me know."

Forty-Three . . .

At the camp of the Salotai, Thais was surprised to find Malek in the crowd that welcomed their arrival. The Ooma gave him a bear hug.

"I told you that my scouting days are over, friend. But in these Cold Days, I grew tired of sitting at home. So we are wintering with the Salotai."

"You are most wanted and respected," Andar spoke up.

"Did Keal travel with you?" Mira asked.

"She did." Malek smiled down at Shana, bundled in her winter suit of sheep down. "And Lian is here. Lian has been all excitement waiting to see Shana again."

Mira spotted Keal in the crowd and ran up to her. *My friend!* She signed. *You are on an adventure at last.*

I couldn't wait to see you, Mira. And your mountains. I have made many friends in this village. I like living in a cave. Very warm.

The times are strange; great fear and great hope.

And we will fight together.

Mira smiled. *We fight from a distance. Atlatls and sling-stones. To beat the Menkala is to strike from a distance and stay away from them. It will be to kill them from afar.*

I will fight to the death, Keal signed. *The women here—they all want to fight.*

That could be the difference.

They want to fight because of you.

Mira stared away. The brittle winter air had pine in it, and it was fresh and cold. She looked around at the Ooma women and girls who were watching her. *There is some of me,* she signed. *That wants the world to stay, and that I could live a life of peace with my mate and my children. But there is some of me that wants war, that craves it.*

Adventure! Keal signed. *We all die, my friend. Why not die on an adventure?*

Thais was surprised that the Ooma had seen in the great plains fire what he had:

"I have instructed my warriors exactly that," Malek said. "That if we may find ourselves close to the enemy; and if the wind blows out of the south, as it so often does in the Long Days—we set the grass afire so that it races toward the enemy. We have practiced this."

"Well there you are," Golthis said. "And if it blows from the west, we should burn the enemy down."

"The fire would kill women and children," Andar said. "It would kill animals; it would kill bison. It would kill those plains. I saw where it had burned, and it was a land of blackness where nothing lived and nothing stirred."

"They would kill our lands," Golthis said. "They would burn our women and children without a thought. I have seen what they did to the Palotai."

"This is one thing that we must discuss," said Thais. "Whether it can be done, or will be done, we should at least plan for it. It might be a weapon that ends the Menkala forever. But we must take this idea to the Paw-Nee, for they know what wildfires can do; and I believe it would be an act very much against their gods. It could race across the Short Hills and rage across their own lands." He looked at Malek. "And even your lands, if the winds shift."

To Thais's surprise, Malek said, "We have already spoken to the Paw-Nee of this. They saw the smoke of the great fire last season, and they retreated quickly from it. They have seen it many times in their own lands."

"You are in contact with the Paw-Nee?" Thais asked.

"They send scouts south and we send scouts north to meet them."

Thais smiled. He smelled the silvery air that lay over the snow. He could smell the piney mountains and fresh water of the river. He smelled victory. "What say they?" he asked.

"They say that if such a strategy is used, they must know if it is used by you, from the west. So that they can retreat from it east. If we start the fire in the south wind, it will not endanger their lands. And unless it leaps the Flat River, it will not reach any of the north tribes."

"The enemy must be close," Thais said. "Otherwise we do not trap them in the flames, we only push them toward one of our allies."

"The Paw-Nee know this," Malek said. "If they see smoke from the west, they are prepared to retreat and battle the escaping Menkala."

"My spies tell me that they are many," Golthis said. "And that they do not often back away from battle."

"The Menkala might expect this," Andar said.

"That would not matter," said Thais. "If our luck puts us in the right place, they could not stop it. And they would never start a fire, even to send it at us. Anyway the wind might blow from the north or the west or the south. But on the Short Hills, it never blows from the east; and the enemy and the friend will be east of us. It is something worth considering. More important is that we all move against the Menkala at once, from every side if possible. They will think the Paw-Nee their greatest threat, and if a wild fire chases them away from the battlefield, it may be unwise. This will be no small battle, My Comrades: it will be spread out over a great distance. The Menkala will try to pick the fields to fight on, so we must be patient. If we invade their lands it will inflame them; that will be the time for patience."

"We know this is true," said Malek. "We defeated them by backing away from them."

"This is not cowardice," Thais said, shooting Golthis a look. "It is wisdom."

They stayed many days at the Salotai camp. It was a mild winter, and no snow storms bothered the glittering quiet days. Lian and Shana played along the icy river, the two wolves watching out for them. Shana had given the Salotai children one of the puppies, and they had named her Spots, due to her mottled grey and cream coat. She was a feisty pup, and the Salotai children delighted in tossing rawhide toys for her to fetch. She scampered around the Salotai camp, and everyone gave her treats.

"That one will become a very fat wolf," Thais said, watching the children play. Lian had already picked up river tongue and could speak almost as well as Shana. They chattered together like two excited chipmuncks. "The Salotai are spoiling that pup."

"She is a pup of the Hosho Dona," Mira said. "When the Salotai see Dona, they make signs. They believe her to be great magic."

"A fat spoiled dog is a fat spoiled dog," Thais said.

"When must we return home?" Mira asked.

"Two days from now." Thais smelled the air. "These Cold Days are passing in peace. There has been little snow in the Short Hills."

"What does that mean?"

"It might be the Dryness. No snow, no rain. It is the seasons where the plains turn dry, rivers lose their water and every creature out there suffers."

"That will help us, when the war comes?"

"Yes, it will." Thais put his arm around her and kissed her. "My love; is there any way I can make you stay away from what is to come?"

"No."

"Not even for Shana?"

"No. Shana will stay with Jella at the Conai village. I go to war with my mate."

"Many woman warriors will be with us."

"Keal took me down the river and showed me what she can do with her sling. I could not believe my eyes."

"Our enemies laugh at such a weapon," Thais said. "It may be that we crush their laughs, and their jaws." He patted Mira's soft brown hair. "They want to fight because of you, My Love. You have shown them that women can fight and be in the songs."

Mira blushed. "It is only because I fight with the great Thais."

Thais smiled. "I think it is because you were born to fight the world."

Forty-Four . . .

Winter was always brutal on the plains. The sun would not warm the earth, no mountains stood against the bitter wind. There were days when the wind would kill a man in minutes. Though there was little snow this season, the bison died in record numbers; the wild fire last summer had scorched grass from the Short Hills, and there was no winter forage for the great beasts. Karas stared out from his teepee, knowing that his people were at their weakest. Daily Regga, the High Priest, grown mad from god herbs, dragged unbelievers into the cruel snow to behead them in front of the throngs who worshipped the God Stone. They wanted blood; somehow they needed blood. Warriors squatted in their teepees and grumbled, and only wanted the end of the Cold Days, when they could fight again. He knew that they were growing tired of the endless rituals and blood-letting that Regga commanded. They were warriors—clear-eyed— and they could see the cloudy eyes of the Mogan. They were warriors; they could sense the enemies gathering round them, to strike when the Cold Days were over.

It was said that the women of the enemy tribes were training for war alongside their men. The One God said that this was a great sin, to allow women into that hallowed realm of men. Regga had cackled when he learned that the enemies were training women to be warriors; that they were making women the equal of men. This was a sign, he said, that the enemies were weak and desperate. He waved off the grim songs that had come to the fires of the Menkala; of the mate of Thais and how she had fought and killed; how she had killed bison, how she had killed Menkala warriors; how she had killed the sacred mammoths. A woman—a woman with a Hosho Dona at her side. A fierce and dangerous woman, the mate of Thais. How could it be, Regga asked the believers, that women could be the equal of men?

The Menkala women all bowed their heads to the God Stone. But their eyes were troubled. They had heard the songs of Mira, of Blue Bird; they knew of the White Wolf of the Tolai, the female wolf. Women who fought with men, women who spoke their minds. The One God had commanded that they be slaves to men; that women must be slaves because women were weak. But they saw women beyond their tribes who were not weak. Songs came even to the Menkala of women who fought and hunted and were the equal of men. The God Stone had not destroyed these women, as Mogan Regga said it would. Wolves were evil beasts, the God Stone said; creatures to be destroyed. But they had heard tales of the Hosho Dona, and the God Stone had not destroyed her. The women of the Menkala began to see that they did not have to be the slaves of men.

Winter was always brutal on the plains. The sun was pale yellow, but it gave nothing to the world. Snow fell on the blackened grass where the great fire had burned. The slaves of the Menkala died by the dozens in the cold wind. The bison were easy to harvest; they died shivering in the cold air, and the Menkala butchered them and roasted them over campfires. Karas stared out at the winter day. Nekena was dead, swallowed by the great mountains of the west. Word had come from spies that Zianna, the Witch of the Conai, was dead. She who the tales said could never die.

Karas could not understand this changing of the world. How the God Stone had disrupted the ageless rhythms of life. Now came the Dryness to the plains. In some ways it favored the Menkala: their slaves found dead bison easily, and warriors were fed well. No blizzards roared out of the west mountains. What little snow that came out of the skies was dry sprinkle. These Cold Days were still and crackling. The world seemed fixed in quiet.

Regga preached that the One God was favoring His people, giving the warriors time to rest and eat and grow strong in order to face the coming war. To let them recover from the ill-fated and wasted march to the desert. Karas was well aware of the strategy his brother planned: to unleash all the enemies of the Menkala in a war to end all. Thais would have been chieftain of the south, had he not angered the gods. How strange his destiny had turned out from that moment.

Karas was coming to know that the Stone from Heaven could not prevent the tribes of men from hunting the bison. Those beasts that made a sea of black across the lands of the Menkala. It was a new life blood to the tribes of men; the great impossible treasure of the plains. Those tribes who had hunted beyond memory the stringy antelope and skinny deer, to discover the great bison herd. Their eyes coming open to this miracle that wandered the plains.

Karas did not truly know his brother—not as Regga did, who had been Thais's friend and companion in the old days. But the God Stone had fully corrupted Regga; he was now lost in belief, dazed in visions, drunk on the blood of sacrifices, of those he claimed did not believe. He was becoming mad with the power of fear. And beyond the Short Hills the enemy gathered from all directions. Ever the Menkala had slain their enemies, one tribe and the next. This was different. This was truly the changing of the world.

Dry snow lay on the plains. The Flat River flowed under cracked ice. A white horizon stepped up to the vast mountains that took the breath and strength from warriors. Karas had always believed that to destroy his brother and the growing might of the mountain tribes, the war would have to be here, where Menkala had been fighting beyond memory; where they could not be defeated. Thais would lead his people here, at the end of the Cold Days. They would come to fight for the bison; they would attack with songs in their minds: of Thais the Leader; of the Giant of the Conai, Golthis. Of the woman who walks with wolves, the woman who went into battle and put strange fear into the enemy; the woman who walks with the Hosho Dona. Karas knew what Thais knew: the great war would not be about gods. It was simply a war for the bison.

Below the great sandstone spire, and around the slave-built temple of the God Stone the snow was red. Blood of sacrifices. Slaves who talked back, women who wandered out of their teepee and showed themselves to men, those who in any way questioned the God Stone. Regga spilled blood for cheering people. But fear ruled the Menkala.

Karas sensed it, he smelled it. Regga knew the power Thais had brought to the enemy. It was freedom. And freedom was the mortal enemy of the God Stone. It was what had ignited the hopeless slave rebellion. It was what made the distant tribes dare the wrath of the Menkala.

Forty-Five . . .

In these Cold Days Mira had nightmares about the Menkala: of war and blood and fire. She often woke in the middle of the night trembling and gasping at the vision of those tattooed monsters. When she again slept, and the sun woke her, still she trembled. The Long Day stepped ever closer, a demon-face at the end of the Cold Days.

"There are many having bad dreams as the Long Day approaches," Thais said to her.

"It's strange," Mira said. "But just when these dreams are at their worst, I hear a strange song."

"A song."

"Yes . . . well not really a song but a simple melody. I hear a strange melody and it calms me."

Thais studied her. "Can you remember the song? Can you hum it for me?"

"I'll try." Mira frowned. She had a good voice, and she had crafted many songs for the great hall; but she was embarrassed for some reason. "It was just a strange melody from a bad dream. I don't know if I can remember it."

"Will you try?"

Tentatively, Mira searched her memory. Slowly the melody came to her lips; it was not complicated, only a few notes. Yet as she hummed it, the music in her dreams, she grew calm, and was surprised at how haunting and beautiful it sounded to her undreaming ears.

Thais listened closely, a smile growing on his face. "Very beautiful, Mira," he said. "Another weapon, the most beautiful."

"A weapon?"

"Yes. You must teach this song to Keal and you must sing it wherever we go, and have it spread to all the tribes. This will become our song!"

"It's not a song," she said. "It's only like a short bird's call."

"Perfect," Thais said. "That will become our song; let me hear it again."

Mira hummed the simple melody, then looked at her mate. "It's not a war song. One that would rally warriors and inspire armies."

"I believe it is," Thais said. "And we must teach it to everyone."

"How can a little melody be a weapon?"

"It may help to unite us, all of us; a tune to remind us that we are not alone."

"It's not a war melody."

"It soothes you in your terror; it will soothe others. Believe me, Love, it is a beautiful melody that stays in the ears. Maybe there was a reason it came to you in a dream."

"You never sing the songs of your tribe," she said.

"They were not like the songs of the mountains. They were savage songs; there was no beauty in them. Not like this song."

Thais was right: Mira taught the simple melody to all of the Salotai. She taught it to Keal and Lian to take back to their people. In the final months of the Cold Days the melody spread from tribe to tribe. It was on the lips of warriors and pot-makers; of Chieftain and Shaman. Of children and aged. The simple melody became a uniting sound; it spread with astonishing speed because it was the language of them all.

When the Long Day approached, and ice dribbled from mountain pines, the melody was heard, whistled and hummed and sung in every tribe that prepared their warriors for the Long Day. It calmed, it inspired, it somehow lifted the heart; it gave a plaintive courage and resolve to those who would venture out of their lands and into the world of war. The warriors had trained hard, and they knew that they must move as one when the terrible hour arrived. Thais, knowing the Menkala more than anyone, had drawn up strategies for all the forces that would move against the enemy.

And one last weapon he discussed with the mountain tribes: "Kandala," he said. "A giant stampede of bison that would tear an army to shreds. We know how to do this."

It would have been good to have more time; but the Long Day was near, Mira's nightmares grew ever darker; and one morning it was time to march to war.

THE LONG DAY . . .

Forty-Six . . .

"Mama—why do you have to go away!" Shana cried.

Mira held her and let her cry herself out. "Oh, My Papoose. I must go with your daddy to the east where there are no mountains. Do you remember those lands, Shana?"

"Yes!" Shana bawled against her, and Mira felt her heart break. "I want to go too!"

"No, you cannot. Now brush tears and be brave."

"Don't leave me, Mama!"

"Shana—I must. But only for a little while. Then I will be back, and Daddy will be back. You must stay here with the Salotai and help Jella care for little Tintia."

"Will Wolf and Dona stay?"

"No. They must go with us. Their two puppies will stay with you, but Wolf and Dona must go with us."

"Where, Mama!"

"You know where, I have told you: we must go to war. These young Salotai and Emotai and Conai; and our brave Tolai—you know what they have been training for, with the rocks and the arrows. We must fight those who want to hurt us—to hurt you. Dona and Wolf go also to protect the tribe; because they are warrior wolves. You must brush tears and make me proud of you. You have to be brave, Shana."

"What is war, Mama!" Shana could not stop crying.

"I have told you what it is, and so has Daddy. You know what it is."

"What if you get hurt, Mama! What if you die!"

"Stop your crying. I will be protected by Wolf and Dona. I will return to you with a smile, My Papoose; and so will your Dasha. Now stop your crying. You have the puppies we gave to Jella; you have all of your friends here; you have all of your toys."

"I have my dolls Andar made for me."

"And Keane made you that toy with the twine and wood."

"I have that."

"And Keane made you that little spear that you can throw."

"I have that. But the boys always want to throw it."

"Then you must share. You have many toys, Papoose."

"I brought the wood bison Andar carved for me and gave me on the Short Day."

"See all the toys you've been given, Shana? And how many love you?"

"I named my wood bison Brave," Shana said, finally snuffling herself out of tears.

"A good name," Mira said. "Now we must say goodbye, My Papoose. But only for a little while."

"Oh, Mama!" Shana went back to crying against her mother.

Mira looked east, where a morning mist lay over the mountains, a mild, silver veil. Such peace—such beautiful peace.

Now war entered the world. Hatred poisoned all the lands of men. The young warrior Andar stared out at the gathering army of the Salotai. He followed Thais because Thais was so like him; eager to fight the world, come what may. Thais wanted this great war; he needed it. At the same time, Mira—the woman of the wolf—had inspired countless women to become warriors and to fight the monsters. Perhaps that was the destiny of humans, to forever struggle against one another. To fight or die.

Andar did not put a great store in the God Stone. As Thais had pointed out, the gods throw stones at the world every night. Why should one be more important? Andar did not believe there was only one god. The gods, each with a power on the earth, lived in the sparkling sky. At night the sky-sparkles were the campfires of those beings. Other gods ruled the day and slept at night. And then the night gods appeared like calm whispers.

He knew in his heart that this great war was not truly about gods. The enemy—the Menkala—thought that they would be fighting for a One God they called Menka. The belief united them in a cause, a holy crusade of death and slavery that would spill out of these Short Hills and into all lands—if it were not stopped here and now. Thais knew this. Despite his youth, Andar had studied the Menkala many times, from a hiding place. Now he had crossed the east plains to the tribes of the Paw-Nee that would face the main wrath of the Menkala.

Forty-Seven . . .

The longest day of the year had always been a day of feast and celebration, for all tribes. The Menkala celebrated the Long Day as most tribes did; feasting and dancing and singing far into the bonfire night. To rejoice at the end of the Cold Days; to smell summer wind and to see the snow melt away under the sun.

Ever the tribes of the river would celebrate the Long Day. Mira would sit in the bright sunlight on the day the great god of the sun stayed into the night with his people. Then she would help her mother with the feast. And her best friend Adela would scamper up to the caves and shake Mira in her excitement.

Now she stared out of the Lion Pass on another day in another time.

Drums of the Long Day, summoning the tribes to the celebration. Pounding echoes on walls of mountain. How those sounds would thrill Mira in her girlhood, when her mother was alive; when Adela was alive.

Now she could not hear the drums of the Tolai. It didn't matter; there were no celebrations this season. No one welcomed the end of the Cold Days. The people in this part of North America dreaded the Long Day, when all fears would be unleashed. They saw their young march away toward the frightening Short Hills. They watched the world change. The older mountain people had never imagined war. They had never imagined a Long Day like this.

"It was always coming," Thais said. "The wars of men were always coming. I wish it were not so—but it is."

Mira pinched him on the leg. "What about the wars of women?"

He smiled and kissed her. They were standing at the Lion Pass that led down into the hills of grass. The green world folded away beyond the eyes. The vast panorama grew dark purple shadows as evening turned to night.

"The enemy is out there," Thais said. "Not far from us. I hope we don't need a miracle."

"Let it be a miracle," Mira said.

"It will be terrible, My Love. I wish that you had stayed behind with Jella and Shana. This war—it will be terrible."

"The girls and women who sing of me, in the campfires; who make me the woman of the wolf . . . they march to fight! How can they fight if I do not fight?"

Thais smiled at her. "It is only that I could not live without you."

Mira stared out of the Lion Cave Pass at those Short Hills that made a canvas in her nightmares. Hills that went beyond to the flat lands of the Paw-Nee. Between, controlling the great bison herd, the enemy. Tatooed beings with only hate and savagery in their hearts.

She no longer cried at the terrible times that had come. It was only now to go to war, to fight and kill the monsters, or to die.

"The gods fight," she said, as Thais stroked her hair. "The gods always fight."

"Yes, My Love." Thais stared out at the lands of his early tribe. Those hills of grass and clay he had sprinted across and lived off of, and conquered and where he had become an animal. He did not know how it had ever come to this moment—only that it had. He sensed that his brother Karas was down there leading the Menkala force. It had always haunted Thais that Karas was his brother, and they had always hated each other. Their father had been one of the Menkala chieftains, and he had one day taken Thais aside and said: "Your brother is weaker than you. You will be chieftain of the Menkala—not him."

And then I said that there were no gods. Thais smiled at the Short Hills, at the fate that had brought him to Mira and Shana and the Tolai.

Mira was looking at him. "My Mate—is there anything to smile about?"

"I'm not sure."

As they stood together and stared down out of the Lion Pass; fires began twinkling in the far-off plains. The Menkala waiting for them. Wanting to kill them, to destroy all of them. And then to invade their mountains, where Shana was.

"There they are, My Love," Thais said.

"They are many," said Mira, petting the white wolf Dona, who sat at her side.

"Our scouts say that all tribes are in place to attack them. We can win; but it will be a very bloody thing."

Mira shuddered against him. They did not seem real, the days that had brought them to this. Days marching to this one day of reckoning. She stared out at the land she had marveled at many seasons ago; a land that had only been in songs.

Out there the warriors of the world were moving into the Short Hills where great creatures, men and animal, stalked the world. She could smell the minty fragrance of her beloved mountains. The wind that flowed down cold and clean from the far peaks. She petted Wolf left of her and Dona right of her. She stared down at those twinkling campfires on the Short Hills.

"I think of Shana," she said to her mate.

"I do too."

"I wish the times were not as they are. I wish they were as they used to be."

"I do too, Love." Thais stroked her hair. "It is only now to end this and try to find peace."

"If we find peace—will it last?"

"Probably not. There will always be war."

"There are so few of us here." Mira stared down from the Lion Pass. "What if they send a force up here to attack us?"

"We would be in a lot of trouble."

"Tomorrow is the Long Day." Mira petted Wolf and Dona. "Will they believe our ruse?"

"I think so. We have prepared as best we could. This was always meant to be, Mira."

"I know that. Had you come to me, or had you not— this was always meant to be." She kissed his hard, bristled face. "I am glad you came to me."

Forty-Eight . . .

Karas stared up at the Lion Pass, where the forces of the mountain people had gathered. His spine tingled when he marveled that they were going to do what he had always wanted them to do: to march down into the lands of the Menkala.

Yet he did not want this war. It was foolish; it was a waste. The Menkala had made too many enemies, all to attack in distant places on the morrow, the Long Day. If this was lost, the Menkala would be no more. The God Stone had united North and South Menkala. Karas did not know how the God Stone—no bigger than a fist—had come from the heavens. He did not doubt its magic; he had seen it arrive with his eyes. It had to mean something.

Karas stared at the campfires that blazed on the Lion Pass. They must boast 800 or so to his 600. Even at this distance he could hear their yells and songs as they made fire in the blood and prepared for battle. The Long Day War would make tales and songs far into the dark future. It would be the War of the Tribes as their empire was attacked from many distant directions, by Ooma and Crow and the far Paw-Nee.

The Menkala warriors, painted in grotesque images of violence and death, had been ordered to keep quiet and make few campfires. Their eyes glowed at the fires on the Lion Pass, the fires of the invaders. Karas had been sickened by the blood and gore committed at the Temple of the Stone, what was done to women and children, to please Menka, to bless this war. It was as if the God's madness ruled the Mogan's death need. He alone could speak to Menka, the One God. Warriors marched with the god in their hearts; Regga had told them that they could not be defeated, that Menka had commanded that they purify the world.

But Karas was not sure of victory, though he had wanted this; it was not the Menkala way of war; ever they had attacked and killed and burned their enemies. The enemies had never before come to them. Karas felt them gathering; powerful tribes who would fight to the death for the bison, God Stone or not. Great victories, which Regga expected, would bring hoards of slaves to the Menkala; it would bring a paradise to the Menkala. When the purification of the world was complete, there would never again be cold, hunger, want. It was pleasing to believe.

Karas watched his warriors gather at the base of the Lion Pass. Two days ago he had watched another army march south to confront the Ooma; he had watched the largest army march east toward the dreaded Paw-Nee. The united forces of the North and South Menkala were scattered and out-numbered; and Karas, marching with the west army, knew the mind of his brother. This would be a war of annihilation; there could be no sharing the bison herd with enemy tribes: the bison would only make them stronger and more dangerous.

This army would fight on the most familiar ground. They carried spears, atlatls and stone knives. Each warrior carried bars of pemmican and a gourd of water. Their leather moccasins rose to just below the knees, their war shirts and leggings, like their faces, were painted in fierce colors. It was to put fear into the enemy; and as Karas inspected them, his confidence rose. The winter had been mild, and the Menkala were well-fed and strong. When the force of 600 had come across the path of the Great Fire a cheer erupted. Above them in the distance stood the mountains and the Lion Pass. Tomorrow was the Long Day, when the mountain forces would march down to battle.

Forty-Nine . . .

Thais had no intention of marching down from the Lion Pass. The force he had brought here was only to start the many campfires and pretend to be the main army; a diversion. Golthis was leading the main forces silently south and east. In the darkness of this night, Thais would try to steal away and lead this smaller force northward to a pass Andar had discovered, one that would take them down behind the Menkala to meet with the main Crow army coming from the north. His men up here made a great deal of noise and wandered continually across the campfires to create the illusion of an army. It seemed to be working.

Mira shivered looking down at the fires of the Menkala. Countless times, as the Long Day approached, she had tried to imagine how this thing would be. Now it seemed unreal. She was weary, but knew that she could not sleep; even now this force was preparing to march toward the Crow army, and all would march through the darkness.

"My brother's army will not sleep this night." Thais studied the distant campfires on the Short Hills. They will be expecting a night attack."

The force at the Lion Pass set out quickly northward, their scouts keeping an eye on the enemy campfires on the plains. Very soon the Ooma and the Paw-nee would be in positions to face their own armies. Mira followed the warriors north into lands that were new to her eyes. The stars seemed to throb in the night, and she willed the weariness out of her mind and body. They traveled quickly, Wolf and Dona staying close to her and Thais. They pushed on downward until, at a thin path that dropped sharply, Mira heard a familiar melody whistled from below; her song, the one that came to her in her dreams. Thais whistled the tune back, and soon a scout appeared and motioned them down the path.

"This is a path?" Mira clutched Thais's arm.

"Not much of one."

"We wander far from our army. Will the Crow conquer the God Stone?"

"They should. They have every advantage, and they are no strangers to warfare. If all goes to plan, the Crow attack will be a complete surprise. With luck, the Menkala army of my brother will stay there in the valley for at least a day."

"I will be afraid meeting those Crow."

"It's necessary."

"Some of them fear the God Stone; their chieftain wants them to see us and to see the White Wolf. It will inspire them seeing you at the Great Spire and the new temple. Now save your lungs and concentrate, Mira; this path is very dangerous."

It was a twisting, frightening steep walkway where unseen stones bulged underfoot, and granite walls towered on either side of them. Even Wolf and Dona stepped carefully. Moonlight flickered over boulders and stunted cacti; fragrant bushes scratched the wind. Terrain not unlike the desert of the Ooma. It seemed forever until the steepness leveled out and they were at last in the Short Hills. Mira's aching body was grateful when Thais called a rest on a tall hill. Mira stared at the sparkling stars, the bright full moon. How had it ever come to this?

She sat down on the soft grass and massaged her legs. The Menkala fires, now south of them, were thankfully lost in the distance. Her mate seemed pleased.

"I believe we have fooled them and pinned them there for at least a day. If we have not fooled them into thinking an attack will come from the Lion Pass, we could be in real trouble. This force must travel fast. We need to assure the Crow that our armies are out there to support them and meet them for battle at the Sand Lake. Our first goal is to make confusion."

They marched east over the land of hills and grass, but Mira grew less tense. The wind tonight was very sweet. Thais was all business; his eyes darted sharply to the south.

He gently touched her hand. "Now it is only to keep our minds on what we have to do."

"It was never meant to begin on the Long Day."

"Hopefully it will keep the enemy confused and at their places—for a while. The day after tomorrow some time you will see the Great Spire. We hope the Crow will be attacking that place with a huge force, because it is a forbidden place; it is weakly defended. Groups of Crow slaves are farther out in the hills, guarded by only a few Menkala; we leave them to deal with their tormentors."

"All this just so they can see Dona."

"This way we have come just so they could see Dona?"

"And you. The Crow warriors are much like the Menkala; they paint themselves and wear feathers to show how many they have killed. They were a people who lived farther north. When they heard of the bison they began to steal across the flat river, just as we began stealing out of the mountains—to harvest as much as possible, then escape. They are wild and fierce, what I have seen of them. If they do not join us attacking Karas, it will leave us in a very bad place. When you go into their camp they will stare at you and maybe scowl at you; you have come to their fires in songs. And they question such tales of a woman. Keep Dona close to you, and it is important that you show no fear. They want to know us, but they do not quite trust us. We will reassure them that our armies are truly out there, and prepared to fight the Menkala. Show them no fear, Mira. Show no fear when you see the thing they hold up to you. At that moment, stay calm and brave. If Dona or Wolf growl, that will be for the better. But have nothing in your face when you see the thing that will be shown to you."

Mira stared away, her heart hammering suddenly. "The God Stone!"

Fifty . . .

"There it is, My Love," Thais said.

Mira stared up at the great sandstone spear that went so far into the sky. Thais had told her about it, and she dreamed that one day she could see such a thing. But not like this.

Below this hill was a great orgy of flames and violence. Screams and grunts and animal cries echoed across the hills. She held onto Thais as a scout gave a fire signal and got one back. Thais looked down at the spectacle: "They have over-run this garrison of Menkala. The enemy believed that no one would attack the shrine."

"By the gods!" Mira tried to hold onto her courage. But she did not want to go down there, where that great spear stood, rooted in giant boulders. Below which was death and savagery: screams, cries, yells. Figures danced in crazy triumphant against the fire flames. "How can a spire of rock rise like that out this land?" she asked.

Thais chuckled. "That I can't answer, My Love. When I was a boy we all had to make a journey to this place to pray to the gods. It is a very holy place to the Menkala; one that my old friend Regga used to his advantage. Ever he was fighting for power. I wonder if he is down there."

Mira watched the carnage rage at the base of the spire; the flames and smoke. "Why do we not fight, Love?"

"This one is for the Crow. No tribe has suffered more than them at the hands of the Menkala. When we get another signal, we will go down there."

It was a humid night, and Mira welcomed the warm wind. It wasn't long before the battle was over; she could see Menkala being herded across the bonfires. She could just make out the shape of the temple she had heard of, a man-made cave. Keal had told her of some desert tribes who were very skillful builders of stone caves. Did slaves of these people build that temple? She sat down on the grass and rubbed Wolf and Dona. She must not fear those warriors, their screams, their paint.

"Before this is over," Thais said. "You will get your chance to fight."

"What will happen to them when they take the God Stone?"

"I hope it will cause my brother to think with his rage."

Finally was the signal and Mira, clinging to Thais, followed a Crow scout down into the valley of the great spire. As she followed Thais down among the Crow warriors, Mira expected more yells and chants; but the crowd grew quiet. Wolf and Dona barked at the warriors, as they made a strange savage corridor. She held onto Thais and walked with him, her eyes as cold as she could make them. She tried not to flinch at the sight of Crow warriors surrounding captured Menkala, then stabbing them to death and throwing them onto piles of dead. This is war, she thought, making her own eyes dead.

"Keep Dona close to you," Thais whispered.

Mira looked around at the white eyes of the Crow warriors that seemed to glow out of the dark painted faces. Eyes that kept flickering down to stare at Dona. They approached the Crow Chieftain and Thais nodded to him. The chieftain nodded back. He was a little younger than her father, Mira thought; and like her father, he had wise eyes. He wore a great head dress of feathers.

The Crow Chieftain looked down at Dona, who squatted, worried and alert, between Mira and Thais. *The Hosho Dona,* he signed.

"This is Man of the Water, Chief of the Crow People," Thais said to Mira. *This is my mate. Her name is Mira.*

We all know of Mira: Woman of the Wolves. Suddenly the chieftain grinned at her, displaying a row of corn-colored teeth, and Mira smiled back.

I am honored to meet you, she signed. She glanced down as the Crow chieftain opened his fist and showed her the God Stone. It was small and glistening black. The stone that had come from the One God; the Stone from Heaven that had brought all of this to the world.

She looked into the eyes of Man of the Water and tapped her fist to her heart.

He smiled. Then he turned to Thais: *What of this?*

This belongs to your people. The God Stone is yours.

I have heard that you do not believe in the gods.

Tales are not always true, Thais signed.

I question the gods. Man of the Water stared away. *I believe that this is a stone, nothing more.*

The enemy believe it a god. And they will come for it. Even now they might be raging across those hills to attack you. They will not be happy that our army eluded them, and that all their

spies told them about the Long Day are false. They should be
worn out marching back from the Lion Pass.

To Mira's astonishment, Man of the Water extended the
God Stone and offered it to Thais. *Take it,* he signed.

No. It must belong to your people.

So that I can tell them that we now possess some god power?

They will believe it whether you say it or not.

Man of the Water made a hint of a smile. He looked at
Mira, and suddenly his eyes turned dark. He looked down
at Dona, then again fixed Mira with his eyes: *Do you want
to possess this?*

No.

Mira stared as the warriors regained their wildness;
like painted animals that danced and growled and began
once again cheering at the death of each Menkala prisoner.
The Crow lived north of the Great Flat River, and Mira
wondered what lands were up there, how they had shaped
such fierce people. The men had tied their hair into long
black tails adorned with feathers. They wore crude deerskin
vests and deerskin leggings and moccasins of bison skin.
Their main weapon seemed to be the spear; she saw no
warrior with an atlatl.

We must trust your people in this, Man of the Water
signed.

As we must trust you.

*Ever the Menkala have raided our villages. Ever they have
tried to keep us from hunting the bison. Now they come to
destroy us; because of this stone.*

We will not let that happen, Thais signed. *In the morning
our party moves north to the Lake of Sand with the news that
the God Stone has been taken by the Crow, and the temple of*

the enemy is burned. We will attack from the east, where, we hope, it will be unexpected.

We believe in your people; we believe in the White Wolf. Man of the Water made a sign to his warriors. *Before you leave, we have a gift for you.*

The dancing warriors made way. Others carried a strange man forward; he wore what seemed to be the ceremonial robes of a shaman. But he was bloody and broken and near death.

Thais stared at him. "Regga," he said. "Mar tan culu woll san to-bolo (I thought you might have escaped)."

"Saska penta to-bolos (no one ever escapes). Regga's wore a frightening bloody grin. His eyes betrayed madness. "Culu mutay son cee con zar, Thais (You see me at the end, Thais)."

"Mer taicle o nonan kan to meya (I wish it had not come to this)."

"Ye Bela kans al culu (Your brother comes for you)."

"Mer toe."

"Ne Culu zel son kal (Now you watch me die)."

"Non." Thais was offered a spear, but he shook his head. He turned and walked away with Mira. Regga was led to the place of execution, where Mira's stomach turned at the sight and smell of the piles of bodies.

Suddenly Regga looked over his shoulder and yelled out, "Mer gu to con Et Dos! (I go to the One God!)."

Thais led her away; and then they heard a great roar as the High Priest of the Menkala was speared to death.

"It is said that he killed many innocent Crow people," Thais said. "They were sacrificed for that stone." Motioning to the mountain force, he led them out of the Crow camp and into the dark, peaceful prairie.

Mira held his hand, and she was relieved to be away from the terrible massacre, the smoke and fires and death. "He was your friend," she said at last. "Long ago."

"Yes, he was a friend long ago." Thais put his arm around her. "You are shaking, My Love."

"I'm terrified of this place."

They went further away from the madness. The night grew darker. Dona whined at Mira's side.

"She has returned to her homeland," Mira said. "Like you."

Thais stared out at the dark prairie. He carried an unlighted torch to signal to Andar, who was expected at any time. "With luck, he will get here soon. Then we go east, across the bison herd."

"I will like to be away from this terrible place." She stared into the darkness. "How far away are they? The enemy."

"I hope our scouts will arrive to tell us. I hope they are still under the Lion Pass, but I think not. When they find out what happened here, they will come roaring like a storm. Karas wants very much to face our people out here where the mountains cannot protect us. For now, he must return here to attack the Crow, avenge the destruction of their temple and regain the God Stone." Thais pointed southwestward. Under the half-moon Mira could just make out distant shadows stealing quickly away. "Those are Menkala spies.

"Yes, My Love."

"Karas will know soon enough that he must face us and the army of Man of the Water; he will have no choice. He must regain the God Stone. There! Thank the gods, it's the signal."

Mira saw a flicker of fire in the distance. Then it went dark. Again the light, and dark.

"We bed down here for a little while," Thais said. "But soon we all move fast, to our armies. Set up our bed, Mira, and try to get rest." Thais knelt down and sparked flint until his torch caught fire. He held it up and moved a blanket in front of it, then away. As he signaled Andar, he said, "Get rest, Mira. We must leave long before the sun, and you will need strength. Did you eat?"

"I ate a bar of pemmican, and I fed and watered Wolf and Dona."

"Then you must sleep. We go to our battle soon."

"I can't sleep," Mira said. She looked back at the raging fires, the whooping dancing warriors. She tried to close her ears to the savage chanting of the Crow in their unknown language. "I just want to get away from this place."

"I tried to keep you from this."

"I know." Mira saw shadows of men sprinting across the moonlit prairie. Presently she recognized Andar at the front of a brace of warriors.

Thais sighed with relief. "Make our bed and get rest," he ordered. "I will return soon."

She watched him lope into the night to meet Andar and the Salotai scouts. When he returned, she pretended to be asleep. He lay with her, and she could feel the electric energy that was coursing through his body. He had been trained from his mother's stomach to fight and kill, to be a savage. He told her that he hated war, and she believed him. She also believed that he loved it.

"You only pretend to sleep, Mira," he whispered suddenly in her ear.

She rolled over on their blanket, cuffed him and gave him a kiss. "What news does Andar bring?"

"Not good. The enemy is moving this way fast. I had hoped for more time, but they will probably be here in a day. But our armies have made it to the Sand Lake, and they are ready.'

Mira watched six Salotai scouts go loping into the dark hills. "Where do they go?"

"They go to set up a signal line. Our strategy will be a very close thing. Only one thing is certain: the army of my brother is coming here, to the Sand Lake."

Fifty-One . . .

Malek So Conyo, the new chieftain of the Ooma people, stared northward at the black-green prairie. This was where the great fire had raged, and still there was a roasted smell to the wind. He expected his scouts at any time. A large Menkala army camped not far away. The Long Day had passed. It was a sunny day, but far off in the west grey clouds were gathering. He did not know if he wanted rain or not. He only knew that he would not survive this day.

They were dangerously close to the enemy. And Malek knew well the fury of the Lion People. He had positioned the Ooma army under a long brow of hillside that hung over the Grass River. Younger men and women who had never been in battle were positioned along twin hills a half mile south. Malek's mate, the beautiful Keal, waited there with her sling. He thought of her as he stared north across the water. He had led a very restless life, one that took him far and wide across the world. He had said a soft goodbye to her; she saw in his eyes that he would never return.

Many will die, he thought. This day or the next.

It was the next. At dawn the Menkala appeared in force on the north bank of the river. There were at least seven hundred of them, and they immediately sent out savage yells and chants. Malek himself had scouted this force, and he knew that the Menkala leader had no other warriors in the area. In wet times the Grass River would be all but impassable; but these were the days of the Dryness. The Menkala warriors, seeing a force of barely 400 Ooma, leaped into the river and began to cross, screaming out war cries and stabbing the air with their spears.

Malek thanked the gods that his men had trained for this; it would be worth death if his tribe could be rid of the monsters, those who now crossed the Grass River, gnashing their teeth, their painted faces mad with rage, beings made since birth to fly into bloody death and violence. This was not the Ooma way, and Malek saw that many of his men wore masks of fear.

"Wait for the signal!" he called out. The image of Keal faded from his mind. "Let them tire themselves. You have practiced many times for this moment. Now is the time for courage!"

The Ooma warriors fed stones into their slings and stared at the monstrous surge crossing the river to destroy them. The warriors glanced fearfully at Malek, but he waited for the moment. The cries of the Menkala seemed to dominate the air. When they had forded half the river, Malek yelled out, "Slings!"

A sudden fury of stones streaked out at the enemy. The Menkala tried to take the missiles in their shoulders and arms and backs, but many were struck dumb in the head, and fell to their knees in the moving water. As Malek had hoped, the Menkala hesitated under the onslaught of stones. They moved slow in the river stream and many of them fell under the barrage. The rest slogged forward, their painted faces fixed on pure murder. Stones shot into the mass of Menkala warriors, dropping more of them; and when the force made their way into the shallows the Ooma pulled arrows out of their quivers.

"Atlatls!" Malek cried out. A thicket of small spears shot out, and more Menkala fell into the river current. He heard the Menkala chief cry out, and atlatl spears swooshed from the river, bringing Ooma warriors down. Now hate-filled Menkala rushed out of the river and up the dry banks into combat. Malek had hoped for mud at this battle place, but it was a season of dryness and there was nothing more for it.

"Withdraw!" he called to the main force. A host of desert gourds sang notes into the morning air and the Ooma, throwing a last volley of atlatl spears into the charging enemy, turned and ran from them south according to plan. At the canyon half a mile away would be the ambush. Now was the time for Malek to lead his small force of chosen martyrs to buy time—now it was to die.

The Menkala roared forward, sensing victory. They had been born to dive into a fight; they lived to fight. And the sight of an enemy running away from them scalded their blood. They rushed south only wanting to kill, to destroy. But they were spending their energy, and many lay dead in the Grass River. Ahead was the corridor of hills where the Ooma had retreated, and where lurked the young men and women who had trained through the cold days. The Menkala, as expected, ran into the trap. Malek stood at the head of his rear guard and prepared himself for death. Their goal was only to slow the Menkala and kill as many as possible.

Malek stared into the mass of surging Menkala warriors. He had never fought one of them hand to hand. Now he thought of Keal. He knew that his plan would work, after his death. The dwindling assault of Menkala tore into them. A Menkala warrior swung his spear, and Malek ducked down, stabbing with his stone knife. Now was the time of fight and die. His men held firm, taking the fury and momentum of the Menkala front line.

Malek So Conya was a great man, a true warrior. But he was no match for these lions of the plains. He managed to stab this Menkala warrior in the side before Menkala spears stabbed him to death. He fell onto the soft prairie; his eyes saw Ooma warriors die under the storm of Menkala. He thought of Keal.

The Menkala were fewer in number; but having destroyed the Ooma rear guard, they charged ahead toward the retreating Ooma main army. Malek So Conya lay dead on the banks of the Grass River, among the warriors he had known since childhood. His mate, Keal, knelt behind the tall hill with the young men and women and waited to ambush the enemy. She knew in her heart that her mate had been killed holding up the Menkala; he had told her that this would happen. The retreating Ooma army formed a wall beyond the valley of the twin hills. As expected, the Menkala kept their attention only on the Ooma warriors. They were also panting, exhausted. Keal, tears in her eyes and fire in her belly, knelt with the young warriors and fed a stone into her sling. She watched the Menkala warriors stream through the valley between the hills.

She had believed that the monsters would terrify her; but her rage and hatred left no room for fear. She only wanted to destroy. And when the signal gourds sang out, young men and women of the Ooma rose up from the twin hills and sent stone missiles down on the exhausted enemy. The Menkala, looking only forward at the Ooma army, were taken by surprise. They tried to cover their faces, but dozens fell. Strong though they were, the march toward the enemy, the fording of the river and their last charge had finally taken that strength.

A second call of the gourds, and the Ooma warriors charged them. Keal saw with a sad satisfaction the Menkala try to retreat. Her stone bag was empty and her arm ached from working the sling, but she knew that she had felled some of the enemy. The rest fell dead under the onslaught of Ooma spears. Her mate was avenged. She fell to her knees in the grass and cried. Her ears were suddenly filled with the cries of her people—victory cries. She looked up from her mourning to see the young women and men warriors charge down the hill and into the fight. She rose to her feet and screamed at the late morning sun. Her people had triumphed.

"Malek!" She raced down the hill where those who had killed her mate lay dead and dying on the plains.

Fifty-Two . . .

Far to the east, where the Short Hills flattened to a vast distance of grass, the largest Menkala army, 800 strong, marched to meet the invading Paw-Nee. Both tribes had made great warriors, and they were ancient enemies. Like the Menkala, the Paw-Nee were nomadic; they lived in tee-pees and followed the great bison herd, which gave them every item of survival. For the Paw-Nee the bison were life or death. They had disadvantages in this war: no mountains to shield them, no desert to retreat to; a flat battlefield that had given their enemies too many tragic victories.

Yet the Paw-Nee were many, and they had developed an effective spy and scout network that kept them in contact with tribes many leagues distant. They of all people in this center of early North America had the most to gain from this war, and the most to lose. Songs of Blue Bird, the tales of Thais; of Golthis the mountain giant; of Mira, woman of the white wolf and her haunting melody—a dedication to Blue Bird. It was even now being whistled and hummed and sung as a holy song among the Paw-Nee.

They were many, the warriors who gathered near the Flat River to again face the Menkala. More than 1,000 formed in a valley and prepared their weapons. They fought mainly with the spear, stone knife and ax, although atlatls were beginning to find their way into the evolution of the tribe. Days had passed, and no word from the west, where other battles raged.

It was a cool overcast day. In this time of the Dryness the Flat River was only knee-high at its best. They could see the campfires of the Menkala across the river. And the enemy scouts had, of course, been spotted rising out of the grass and dropping back down. These were of the Northern Menkala tribes. The Paw-Nee leader studied their smoke and wondered when they would attack. Never had so many warriors gathered in these lands; it was the dawn of great warfare on the early plains of North America.

He had formed his men into three fluid lines overlapping one another into a rough triangle. His best warriors would take the brunt of the Menkala attack. This enemy, when moving in force, always attacked head on with spears, axes, atlatls, knives, clubs. Grey Hawk, the Paw-Nee general, had pinned his troops against the Flat River, giving them one last message: There could be no withdrawal. This time it was to fight to the death. Grey Hawk would have to lead the front force against the Menkala, and he knew that he would die. He welcomed it because he believed that he would see a final victory for his people not here but from the realm of the Great Spirit. He stared at distant clouds forming in the southwest. The strong southwest wind was maybe bringing a storm in. It is the gods, he believed, preparing for battle in the sky as we prepare on the land.

In those days that we call the New Stone Age death was as mysterious as it ever has been. But life was cruel, often short painful, and death a beacon of peace. For many, like the Menkala, death was the greatest honor. For the Paw-Nee it was a bitter-sweet passage that must be taken today or the next. Better today in battle and songs than tomorrow, of disease or old age. Grey Hawk's father had fallen under a Menkala axes and had earned his way into the songs of the people.

Grey Hawk stared southwest at the smoke of the Menkala army. Too much smoke, he worried. This is a day of battle; but why is it so strange?"

He had fought them before, but not in anything close to this number. It would be a boiling rage of death. Grey Hawk thanked the gods that it had come to this, men battling men on the land, gods battling gods in the sky. Ever was it so, from the first beginning. In this age death was a sad but perfect ending. Grey Hawk did not want to die. He stared south at what was to come. The Menkala studied from birth to imitate the prairie lion. Once, as a youth, Grey Hawk had seen a big powerful hunter taken apart by a lion. They had been on a hunting expedition, and a lion had streaked out of the tall grass and attacked in such power and savagery that Grey Hawk could not believe his eyes. And then dragged away his carcass. No one went after it, because in those days of the Menkala the lion had been holy. The enemy was trained to be like that. This battle would be like that. Grey Hawk did not want to die—life was too sweet—and nothing truly wants to die.

But that was wrong: the Menkala wanted to die. Grey Hawk knew from experience that these warriors charged into death with glory in their eyes. The mountain chieftain Thais knew this; he had been born a Menkala. He knew that this was a weakness. He had sent Grey Hawk a simple message in the cold days: Death for them, not for us. The plan for this great war was wise: for all enemies of the Menkala to ban together to rid the world of them. To attack together in distances that would force the Menkala to spread their warriors far and wide. The force sent to attack the Paw-Nee were the largest. He calmed his heart and tried to prepare his mind and body for the fury of war. There was never much strategy when the Paw-Nee fought Menkala on this wavy plain. Forces attacked like animals, like bull elks launching headlong into their enemies. There would only be more warriors this time.

He was satisfied seeing his thousand kneeling in position; strong, well-trained men who had no fear of violence. For Grey Hawk it would be to lead from the front and kill as many Menkala as the gods allowed, before he fell and his spirit went to them. For this he was ready; but then an unlikely salvation came out of the greying south.

As he was staring away, feeling the last wind on his face, his son Eagle sprinted up the hill to him. "Father, scouts have arrived from the west."

"Is it Andar?"

"Yes, and a brace of warriors from the mountain people."

Grey Hawk went down to meet with them. He tried not to think that his son might die today. He ordered food and beverage for these men who had exhausted their bodies and risked their lives to come here to this valley of death.

"There was a battle south of here," Andar said. "On the Grass River. The Ooma fought a Menkala army. We don't know how it came out."

Grey Hawk looked to the south. "What of your mountain tribes?"

"The Salotai are coming here, quickly as they can. The main army attacks the Menkala near the Great Tower. A Crow army awaits them across the Flat River. The Crow have raided the Menkala temple and captured the God Stone."

Grey Hawk stared away, wondering what that would mean. "The Salotai will be too late," he said.

"I have only a band of scouts. But we will fight with you."

Grey Hawk stared southwestward. "They gather there, they gather quickly. That is a giant of a Menkala army. There will be blood and death all over this valley, maybe tonight. They learned the value of night attack from your people."

"Thais has told me that they probably will not attack you this night. They are too many and it would be too risky."

"When did you speak to Thais?"

"Four moons ago. He will lead the attack against the Menkala who march toward the Crow. He believes they will throw themselves into death because the Crow have the God Stone."

"Still we will prepare for a night attack. What did he say of me?"

"He hopes that you will retreat."

Grey Hawk stared at him. "What! How can we do that?"

Andar waved southwestward. "Can you not see it?"

Grey Hawk saw. "A great storm."

"No. A great fire."

Grey Hawk took a long breath. "A fire."

"We think the Ooma set the fire, in order to destroy the Menkala. The fire moves quickly northeastward, toward you and that Menkala army."

"That is why they've moved so fast." Grey Hawk stared south at what he now knew was smoke. "You and your scouts are to eat, drink, rest and then return to the west."

"The great battle is here," Andar said.

"But not for you. When this battle is over we will need to know how the war ends. You must go to the west and tell the Salotai to turn back. They will not be here in time for this battle. And you must take my son Eagle with you." Grey Hawk gave Andar a meaningful look. "He is a good scout. This is what you Must Do."

Andar bowed. "I will do it. But know, Chieftain, that the fire is rushing toward this valley. The Menkala know this; that is why they must attack you quickly."

Grey Hawk stared toward the enemy. Then he stared beyond, at the grey horizon. His son stood at his side. Suddenly everything came to him: "Order every warrior to withdraw from this valley," he commanded. "We go north, across the river; and we must go fast."

"We cannot run away from the enemy!" Eagle cried out.

Grey Hawk gave his son a volcanic look. "We are not running away, we are defeating them. We have practiced this. You will go west with Andar and meet with the salotai. Now go and see that we are ready to march quickly back across the river."

"Tell them that they are to retreat in the face of the enemy."

"Not retreat from the Menkala. Look out there. We retreat from something much worse."

It was a horror and a salvation. In these times of the Dryness, it was against all sacred rules to start a fire. Once started, a prairie fire raced beyond control and destroyed what was in its way. Even now Grey Hawk saw rabbits scampering away from the darkening distance. He smiled as he saw the way to victory; a dangerous gift from the desert people.

"We must retreat, and retreat fast."

Fifty-Three . . .

"Always before I have felt the gods," Mira said. "This day, I cannot feel the gods."

"You will see them again," Thais said. "We cannot know what the world will bring, how our allies have fared. We can only do our part in this thing."

"This thing that has been in my stomach for so long; so that I can't sleep in peace or feel peace! I wanted adventure; I wanted to see the old tales and songs come to life. Now I feel sick from having too much adventure. I no longer see the world in my dreams. I no longer see my father, or Keane or Shana. I no longer see you in my dreams!"

"What do you see, Love?"

"I only see them."

Mira stared out at the warriors in the distance marching northward toward the Great Spire. The place where she had seen the very God Stone with her eyes. They were the Menkala that had camped below the Lion Cave Pass; those they had fooled into thinking the battle would be there. Below a ridge of short hills stood the armies of her people: the Tolai, the Conai and the Emotai, hidden from those they would soon attack; this time on the rolling green hills.

Their beloved mountains stood away, only as dark forms. Have the gods followed us down here, to protect us?

Down below the hill was a fertile valley, a natural resting place. They had spread items there to make it look like a frantic retreat: food and even weapons were scattered on the plains. And clay jars of water that she had prepared. She did not want to think of the gourds, because their contents violated a sacred vow she had taken before Shaman Haldana when he designated her the Mistress of Herbs, after her mother had died. For in this water was poison. If the Menkala would be terribly thirsty, as Thais insisted, many of them would drink from the gourds. The poison worked slowly, but always killed. It was a sinister way to fight, and she prayed that the gods would forgive them, forgive her. She kept the thought that the fatal juices she had extracted in the mountains might kill the enemy who would kill Shana. Haldana had been shocked at Thais's suggestion to make the poison, and had completely refused to be a party to such murder; but in the end, Shaman Haldana needn't hear about it.

The strategy of the mountain army was to stay out of sight, rest, eat and prepare, and let the Menkala pass on their angry route to the Great Spire, to their temple that had been destroyed by the Crow; to the enemy that had killed the High Priest Regga and stolen the Stone of God. And then to attack them from behind. It would be a close thing, Thais had told her.

Mira lifted her head from the grass and stared away. "They march with a vengeance," she said.

"That is what we want." Thais stroked her sweaty hair. "I wish that you had stayed in the mountains with Shana."

"And that I had not made the poison gourds?"

"If it was a sin to do it, we will find out. But if we are to survive, we have to weaken the lion before we kill it, any way we can."

"I am glad to be here and now, Love. With you and fighting next to you. Peace is not sleeping from the world; it is not being comfortable. It is fighting whatever in the world you have to fight until the gods take you."

"You would have made a great Menkala princess." Thais smiled at her.

"No. Because they hate their women."

Thais stroked her hair. "Soon we will have to fight. Hopefully we can sneak up behind and attack them as the Crow come from the north. However it is, we will have to fight."

"And we will fight together."

Thais held her in the prairie dusk, and felt her heart pounding savagely against him. "When the time comes," he said. "Keep Wolf and Dona close to you."

Karas looked at the strewn items in their path; evidence of a quick retreat. Things a retreating force would leave behind: bedding, weapons, gourds of water. Whoever they were, they had abandoned goods in order to get away from his force. He stared at the north, where, scouts had reported, the great temple had been destroyed, the God Stone taken, Regga killed. I am the leader of the Menkala now, he thought. Now is to fly into total war, and to make the dark and smoky songs of the people.

He called a rest here; his men were exhausted, and he needed them fresh when they came upon the Crow. It was a mild day; the sun smiled behind summer clouds. He feared that Thais was manipulating him, as in the past, when they were children. To tell him he was going to attack from the Lion Pass, and then to vanish like smoke. To draw him toward the God Stone in order to destroy him. His brother was out there waiting. His brother was out there. Long ago Karas had asked his father why he preferred Thais. His father had answered in the Menkala manner: "He is smarter than you. Much smarter."

Karas watched his men open the discarded gourds and drink. They were very thirsty running back to face the Crow. Water was life. Karas stared around at the green Short Hills, sensing danger, but he didn't know what. He must first destroy the Crow and take back the God Stone; that was all that mattered. To cross the river and attack the Crow and to destroy them and take back the God Stone. But where was Thais? Where were the Mountain Tribes?

Karas looked at his men, drinking from the discarded gourds. He blinked his eyes, and his heart caught. "No!" he cried out. "Put down those gourds! Put them down!"

His men all looked at him.

"By the gods!" he said. "They are poison!"

Fifty-Four . . .

Thais sent scouts north to follow the Menkala. They moved in shifts, some going forward and others quickly returning to report the enemy. In the meantime he moved the mountain army across the path of his brother's force. He was relieved to learn that they were continuing to move north, as he had predicted: the Menkala needed water, and so would seek the Sand Lake, where the Crow waited.

The hard part was to time the two attacks from the front and rear, squeezing his brother between the two forces, with the lake at their backs. The Menkala had weakened themselves marching fiercely up from the Lion Pass, and they would reach the lake exhausted. Then would be this battle. He flinched as a familiar paw slammed him on the back. Golthis grinned down at him.

"The spies say that your brother's men are not in good shape. We outnumber them five-to-one, if the Crow keep their promise and don't run away."

"They will attack," Thais said. "We all know that this is win or die."

Golthis waved down the hill at the approaching figure. "This one has already killed 18 by the scouts count. And all with clay gourds." Golthis smiled at Mira, who had come up to join them. She looked at her giant cousin; her eyes were grim.

"What say the scouts?" she asked her mate.

Thais avoided her eyes: "The enemy moves north. They know we are behind them, and their plan will be to attack the Crow, drive them off and then turn to face us. We must trail them close, so that when they battle the Crow we attack."

"What of the poison?" she asked Golthis.

He too avoided her eyes. "They were very thirsty when they came upon our trap."

"You said 18 killed." Mira stared at the north. "By my poison? So far."

"So far."

"We cannot be sure," Thais said.

"I am," Mira said. "And there will be more. I have violated my sacred oath; I have sinned against the gods."

"It could have been the long march that killed them," Golthis said.

"No. They are Menkala. It was my poison that killed them. The witch Zianna tried to warn me."

"Well, so be it. One of them might have killed my Jella, my children! One of them could have killed me had they lived. But I doubt it."

"One of them might have killed Shana." Thais gave her a look. "If we have sinned against the gods, they will punish us."

"The God of this land," Mira said. She stared out at the sweet prairie, the calm and beautiful wind. "What of the God Stone?"

"You saw that very stone," Golthis said. "Did it punish you?"

"I did not touch it," Mira said.

"But your eyes saw it. You beheld the God Stone, the songs will say. And it was offered to you."

"It was a black stone. I saw nothing else. Yet those Menkala out there, they fight to the death for it. They fight for this stone, for what no one can understand."

"Then let the gods decide," Golthis said. "If those demons die by your herbs or my ax, it only matters that they die. That is what I will tell the gods when I meet them."

Mira took a deep breath. She tried to train her heart for this vast and terrible thing; and she wondered what was to come. She had made poison and it was killing people. She had vowed to the gods that she would never do that. It was a terrible sin. Shaman Haldana had refused to make the poison to kill Menkala. He had been angry at Thais for suggesting it.

But I did it, she thought. Men lay dead out there because I poisoned them. She trembled against her mate. Men who would kill Shana. Men who would kill my people.

"We will have to stay close behind them," Thais said. "Send out many scouts and post many sentries. My brother is no fool. He charges against the Crow, but if they retreat he will not follow them across the Flat River; he will turn and come after us. He will only need time to rest his men. And his men will need little rest in order to fight."

"What if those Crow people do not stand?" Mira asked.

Thais smiled fondly at her. "I believe they will. If they do not, if they retreat across the river then we are on our own."

"Still, we'll outnumber those demons," Golthis said. "We can close this thing. We'll finish it for good, and then the bison herd will be for all."

"Why do you want so much to fight, My Cousin?" Mira asked.

"To be in the songs!" Golthis said.

"What if you meet your brother in the battle?" Mira asked her mate.

Thais gave her a dark look: "I have to tell you this: It is the Menkala code that the leader lead," he said. "And to seek out the enemy leader for single combat. This inspires the warriors to fight all the harder. This is what makes the songs."

"Then you will have to be in the front," Mira said. "And to seek out your brother."

"When the time comes—yes. And you must stay back with Wolf and Dona. When the battle reaches you, I know that you will fight."

"But I will not stay back," Mira said. "Where you go to fight, I go. Where you go to fight, Dona goes, and Wolf goes—and let the gods do what They will."

"Oh . . . by the gods, Mira . . ."

"I have longer legs," Golthis said, breaking them apart. "When the time comes, it will be a race to see who will be in front."

Thais smiled. "It's a good thing that Andar is out scouting. You have longer legs, but he's younger and faster than the both of us."

Thais took Mira in his arms and stroked her hair. "You have been in battle with these fighters," he said. "In battle, nothing is certain and nothing is safe. If I meet my brother in this fight, it will be only by chance."

"My ax might find him before you." Golthis made an ugly grin.

The Eastern Paw-Nee knew the signs: the red horizon that was not the setting of the sun; that which could sweep away an army. For all that, the Menkala were approaching the Flat River. They were many miles southwest of the retreating army of Grey Hawk, and he pushed his men reluctantly along. This was the largest force of Paw-Nee ever to take the field in battle, and he almost had a riot on his hands making them retreat. His warriors ached to stand and fight the Menkala; two days before they had come so close to the great battle and they had made their songs. Grey Hawk had told them that they would be in greater songs

"Now they are crying out that we run from the enemy!" his son Eagle said to him. "The leaders say that we are running from Menkala."

"The leaders are not the Chieftain—I am!" Grey Hawk frowned. "Tell them to be wise. They will get their chance to fight that Menkala army; but not now. We do not run away from the enemy, we run away from that fire."

"Scouts say that the Menkala are already crossing the river. They believe they are chasing us away."

"They believe wrong," Grey Hawk said. "If they follow us where I lead them, we will attack and destroy them."

"Where do you lead them, Father?"

"To the Island of the birds."

Mira marched with the army down into the valley where the Menkala had marched. They passed the place where weapons and clothing and her poison water had been strewn; then they made their way north toward the great spear of rock that dominated these plains. How strange and calm the day, a soft wind blowing from the south. Hills and valleys of green grass never seemed to end. She was not weary from all this marching ever northward; what drove her on was more than fear. It was the adventure of life and the facing of death. She thought of her papoose, Shana. She held onto Thais's hand as he pushed the mountain army ever north. Mira looked behind her at the force of mountain warriors that marched in the green distance. She felt a sweet peace in the wind of these Short Hills. It was strange feeling the fragrant wind and knowing she was marching into war. No, she didn't truly feel fear. Ahead of them were many more Menkala warriors dead. Mira studied them and knew that it was her poison that had killed them.

When my songs reach my people, will I become a witch?

Scouts came running from the north: they were coming across enemy bodies. "The rest of their army keeps marching north."

"They believe they can only win by getting back the God Stone," Thais said. "But they know we are behind them. Karas will know when we get too close. But he also knows that he will not be the High Priest unless he gets the God Stone."

"What if they turn and come after us?" Mira asked.

"It would be bad. But I think not: by instinct they can't go back." Thais stared into the cloudy northern sky. "The

God Stone rules them. Our goal is to tire them out and then, with help from the Crow, destroy them."

Presently their marching party came upon dead Menkala lying on either side of the tracks. Mira stared up the green valley and saw bodies of warriors lying everywhere. Death stank the air, and she grew sick, and staggered. "My poison!" she said.

"Mira." Thais grabbed on to her and held her. "This is the way it must be, My Love. We must kill in order to live. That is the way of things."

"I don't want the way of things!" Mira bawled against his chest. "Why does it have to be like this!"

"I don't know. I want what you want, My Love: to live in peace and see Shana grow up, and to maybe have other babies grow up. That is what we fight for."

The mountain tribes were very close to the Menkala, when the enemies reached the Flat River. The trail was strewn with dead warriors, and Karas feared the way ahead. The Menkala stopped to rest in the shadow of the great sandstone spire. The temple that Regga had built was in ruins; the God Stone had been taken by the Crow, who waited north of the Flat River. Karas felt the presence of the mountain tribes on his flank, waiting to attack. Ahead lay the Crow. Would they cross back the Flat River and attack?

My brother has put us into a trap, he thought, feeling an old chill go up his spine. His scouts had seen the mountain army, larger than his own. Karas had watched great warriors fall dead after drinking from the poison gourds. His scouts had seen the white wolf marching with the Tolai. They had heard of a great red horizon in the south, and a distance of smoke. These were the times of war. This was a war that consumed everything; great songs would come from this thing. Karas wanted to kill his brother.

"What will the people who have the God Stone do now?" Mira asked.

Thais held her in the strange prairie sky.

"I only think of Shana, and a better world for her."

"What will they do with the God Stone!"

"I think that they will start worshipping it," he said.

THE END.